SEVEN HEAVENS

Samim Ahmed writes novels, short stories and non-fiction in Bengali. An assistant professor of philosophy in Ramakrishna Mission Vidyamandir, an autonomous post-graduate college, he is the author of eight published books and a regular contributor in reputed dailies in Bengali and English. Samim was born in 1973 in Birbhum district, West Bengal, and grew up in Murshidabad and Kolkata. He lives and writes in Kolkata. *Saat Aasman* ('Seven Heavens') is his first novel.

*

Arunava Sinha translates classic, modern and contemporary Bengali fiction and non-fiction into English. Over twenty-five of his translated works have been published so far. He has won the Crossword translation award twice, for Sankar's *Chowringhee* (2007) and Anita Agnihotri's *Seventeen* (2011), and has been shortlisted for The Independent Foreign Fiction Prize (2009) for his translation of *Chowringhee*. His translations have been published in the UK and the US in English, and in several European and Asian countries through further translation. He was born and brought up in Kolkata, and lives and writes in New Delhi.

SEVEN HEAVENS

Samim Ahmed

Translated by
Arunava Sinha

hachette INDIA

First published in Bengali by Gangchil Publishers in 2012

This translation first published in 2015 by Hachette India
(Registered name: Hachette Book Publishing India Pvt. Ltd)
An Hachette UK company
www.hachetteindia.com

SRD

ISBN 978-93-5009-771-7

Hachette Book Publishing India Pvt. Ltd
4th/5th Floors, Corporate Centre,
Sector 44, Gurgaon 122003, India

Typeset in Garamond 11.5/16
by InoSoft Systems Noida

Printed and bound in India
by Manipal Technologies Limited, Manipal

MIX
Paper from responsible sources
FSC™ C043100

~ *Al-Makam-al-Amin* ~

A SAFE HAVEN

The night before Runa's mother was born Nana – Grandfather – had a dream.

Nana was given to changing the story of the dream every now and then. Sometimes he said that a dervish – a sage – with a flowing salt-and-pepper beard, and wearing a black cloak that covered him from head to toe, had told him, 'Today's the day your family will get an heir.' At other times he claimed that it wasn't a dervish at all; that in fact, he could not make out whether the speaker was a man or a woman. The garments the speaker wore were unusual too, for they made it appear as though the person wearing them had arrived at this unknown village in Bengal from the deserts of Arabia. In a genderless voice the figure had told Nana, 'This day marks the arrival of one who will glorify the name of your family.' In yet another version, a boy-child addressed Nana as 'Abbu'.

Nana's dream had several variations, which kept changing as he grew older. Runa had heard from her Nani – her grandmother – about the various dreams Nana had had before

Runa's Maamu, her mother's older brother, was born. Nana had waited eagerly for a male child and the story of his dreams had changed repeatedly in that time. However, there was one aspect that always remained constant – a male heir found centre stage in every version of his dream.

Nani went into labour one night, and Runa's mother was born when the first light of dawn was streaking across the sky. When her labour pains started, Nani was taken to the designated labour room in the house. When Runa and her siblings grew older they named this room the 'German Hussain Private Nursing Home', after their Nana. At the moment when Nani's pain became excruciating, Nana felt a violent pressure in his bowels. The toilet for men was some distance from the house. On his way there with a pot of water, he noticed a man standing near the pond next to the toilet. In the half-light of dawn Nana identified him as Robin. But, strangely Robin's elbows, knees and ankles were all pointing in the wrong direction. It was as if Robin's head had been set front to back, so that he was looking behind him all the time. Seeing this, Nana could not control his bowels any longer. Runa's brave and arrogant Nana, who was reputed for going for a shit on horseback, was literally left shaking in his shoes. He noticed, even as he began to scream Robin's name, that though the strange spectacle of a man was walking towards him, the distance between them constantly increased.

Nana was found unconscious and brought back home. By then there was a crowd at home, including the ladies of the locality and a midwife, the only Hindu woman present. In these parts, only the women from the tribal Hadi families worked as midwives and she had been keeping a sleepless vigil by Nani's side since the previous evening. By the time Nana was carefully carried into the house, his body limp with fear, Nani had given birth to a child and was lying unconscious in a corner of the labour room.

Word about Nana's ill-health had spread quickly and soon, a doctor well versed in the ancient science of Ayurved had arrived at the house. After all, Nana was the president of the Congress party of the area; he deserved prompt attention. The doctor gave Nana medicines and suggested various nutritious foods to revive his health. Meanwhile, there were other important matters to attend to. The call for prayer – the azaan – had not been sounded after the birth of Nani's child and customarily, neither Nani nor her newborn were allowed to eat a morsel till it was read. Eventually a solution was found. Tentuli, the permanent farmhand of the family, arrived to tend to the cattle. He bathed and offered the azaan, after which an old woman of the neighbourhood smeared honey on the baby's lips. When Nani came, she was given tea with jaggery. Runa's mother was born in the month of Shravan, on a Thursday, the day of the goddess Lakshmi. The year was 1348, according to the Bengali calendar.

As the day progressed, the formidable Maulana Sahib from the neighboring village arrived. Nana was laid on the veranda, on a mattress covered with sheets and the Maulana was given a chair next to him. He enquired in minute details about the events that had taken place and Nana spoke slowly of his dream. He described how he had seen the devil in Robin's form in the half light of the monsoon dawn. He shuddered as he spoke about how Robin's ankles and elbows were turned the wrong way, and shamefully confessed that the sight had resulted in him soiling his cherished Ismail lungi. Hearing this Maulana Sahib said 'You dreamt all this German Mian? These events took place at dawn on Thursday, which means the nymph has set her sights on you. This creature attacks while her victims are relieving themselves. You have to be very careful for the next ten days and even after that because the influence of this jinn-nymph will persist. The evil eye of the nymph will keep troubling you in the form of all kinds of illnesses. Sometimes your back will feel as though it is breaking, at other times it will be an excruciating headache. A thousand nightmares await you because of your ill fortune.'

The matriarch of the family, Runa's great aunt, her Mejo Nani, opened the door a crack and from inside the room asked, 'Maulana Sahib, what is the cure for this? We will spend whatever is required. Just make the arrangements.' The Maulana said, 'Look Bhabijaan, you will have to make an offering to the poor. The offering will have to include a black cock, though a yellow one of moderate size will also do, five spoons of ghee, some mehndi leaves and half a bhari (10 grams) of silver. After this, when the namaz for the ceremony is done, I will send you an amulet. Chant the Bismillah along with three verses, and tie the amulet with a black thread on Bhaisaheb's right arm, above the elbow.

'Very well,' said Mejo Nani and went off to make the necessary arrangements.

Maulana Sahib asked Nana, 'How do you feel now?'

Nana replied, 'So Maulana, are you sure those offerings will cure me? The ayurvedic doctor Ramlochan Kaviraj has prescribed medicines so that I get stronger, shouldn't I be eating all those things you just mentioned to gain strength? What is the point of giving them to the poor? Do you know how much half a bhari of silver costs? I believe in amulets, I know that jinns and nymphs won't dare to come anywhere near me if I wear Khuda's discourse on my body. What is this that you Muslim League people are doing! Is this the faith of my ancestors, is this the dween - the path - that they brought from Arabia! You're not just an ignorant village maulvi; you're a maulana with a degree from a university. How can you say such things? You claim you want Pakistan, but your Hindu habits refuse to go away. Not that it's your fault, each of your leaders has crossed the line, they're worse than infidels!'

Maulana smiled at this barrage of words and the reason was revealed when he spoke. 'Whatever you may say, German Mian, the Muslim League will definitely win. You people can keep saying whatever you like. Their teachings will spread far and wide. Tabligh is inevitable. The faith will spread. The common people will follow the learned leaders, and there are plenty of those among us. Nana said, 'Yes! You have Maulana Thanvi and

Shabbir Usmani, with Jinnah as your head. Naturally you will be uncompromising. This doesn't surprise us. But if the country is split, where will you and I go, abandoning our paternal homes and farmland? That chief leader of yours, Jinnah, do you know what he said? He proclaimed that he will become a martyr for the sake of a Muslim-majority state. It doesn't matter to him if we're murdered. He will let twenty million of us be martyred on the streets and build Pakistan on our corpses.

'Have you heard of Kamal Pasha? The one about whom they said, "*Kamal tune kamal kiya bhai*" (What wonders you have wrought Kamal!) If Mustafa Kamal could create a Turkey, why can't we? The leaders of the Jamiat Ulema-e-Hind have only been badmouthing Jinnah. They refuse to understand that an Islamic state can easily be created with the Muslim-majority provinces, built upon the fundamental faith, laws, jurisprudence and rules of Islam. The Jamiat is now under the control of the Congress. They will go whichever way the Congress wants them to. What you refuse to accept Mian, is that the Congress is the party of the Hindus.

'Do you know what Madani Sahib has said? Those leaders who don't accept Islam want to have Pakistan. Hah! *Ladke lenge Pakistan.* We'll wrest Pakistan by force. Madani has written that if Pakistan is indeed formed, its people will starve. How will its economy be created? Can you tell me that, Maulana? The Jamiat believes that if Pakistan is created it will become the factory of politics for England and Russia someday. I think so too. Can a man like Thanvi understand our plight? The Muslim

League does not have a single alim, a single learned leader, who can divert you from the path that leads away from the Sharia or think of the welfare of our nation, our qaum.'

'Whom do you consider a learned man, German Mian? Madani – you think Madani is learned?' asked Maulana. 'What does he know besides enmity with the British? He is not concerned about Muslims. He will continue his holy war against the British. And the Congress's Abul Kalam Azad! He is neither learned nor a politician. Put all your wise men on one pan of the scales, we'll put our Thanvi Sahib on the other. Check for yourself which way the scales tip. The formation of Pakistan is inevitable.'

At this point Mejo Nana, the second eldest of Runa's great-uncles and the head of the family, entered the room. The eldest brother lived in Dhaka, where he worked at the post office and in his absence Mejo Nana took care of the estate and its affairs.

Calling out to the Maulana, he said, 'Now what, Maulvi? Has Jinnah Sahib come up with anything new? Have you managed to draft German to your cause? I don't think he will join your League or anything. Can your people finance his three horses and Ismail lungis? We do that now. Ha ha ha. While the Mian was seeing a ghost on his way to the toilet, he had a daughter. Now that you're here, why don't you give us a suitable name for her and workout her star sign. We'll look after your needs.'

Suddenly, Nana's face turned pale. He appeared to have seen

Robin again, and seemed ready to repeat his earlier reaction to the vision.

The Maulana said, 'This means the girl was born between five and six in the morning on a Thursday. This girl's astrological sign is Zahul, what you refer to as "Shani" in Bengali. Call her Zahura. She will be quite dark-skinned. But her life will be wrapped around God, her lifespan is long. She will have a lovely voice. Your niece will have a clear heart.'

Mejo Nana took a two-rupee note from his pocket and gave it to the Maulana. 'Keep this,' he said.

In the meantime Tentuli, the permanent farmhand, appeared and asked Maulana Sahib, 'Huzoor, rice was two annas a kilo last monsoon. How could it have become three annas this time? If this is what coarse rice is going to cost, what will happen with fine rice? Ask them to lower the price. We can't afford it. We have children at home, what will we feed them?'

Tentuli had five children. The eldest was eight. He looked after the cows at Mir's house and swept and cleaned the cowshed. For this he got two meals of fermented rice daily. Tentuli couldn't possibly ask his wife to abandon the baby in her arms to work as a maid in other people's houses. His elder son hadn't been home all morning. The six-year-old had gone to the fields and hadn't yet returned. Not that he had gone alone. Many other boys from the village were in the fields as well. The fields were covered with edible taro roots which had sprung up some time ago. The earth had been softened by the monsoon rains, and Tentuli's son was in the fields digging for slugs. If he was lucky, he might get some taro too. But these things were not going to be available every day. Many children from the village came to gather them. Worried about food in the coming days Tentuli called his wife and told her, 'Chhoto Mian had a daughter at dawn today. I read the azaan. Will you go over to their house?'

Tentuli's wife protested furiously, 'I'm finding things difficult with this six-month-old baby here and you want me to work as a maid in that house?'

Tentuli grew nervous. He said, 'Did I ask you to work as a maid? Just pay them visits. Don't people visit one another?' He added with a chuckle, 'Mejo Mian was talking about you.'

This worked almost instantly. Promising to visit the house in the afternoon, Tentuli's wife went indoors. Tentuli shouted after her, 'Ask Mian Sahib for some rice. Just make sure he gives his word. That will be enough.'

Meanwhile, prices had been rising sharply. Not just poor people, but even the small farmers found themselves with their backs to the wall. Even kerosene was unavailable. There was no sugar anywhere; it was difficult to get hold of some, even after paying ten times the price of jaggery. The prices of salt, oil and flour were soaring daily. The money from selling a goat would not pay for a lungi.

The paddy harvest had not been good enough the previous year. Burma was in very bad shape. Wars were raging all over the world, which meant trouble for everyone. Some people in the village had mounds of rice stashed away at home. This was dispatched to the city in bullock-carts late at night, where it was sold at twice or three times the normal price. This rice was supposed to go to Madras, Ceylon and Travancore. The English government couldn't be bothered. The leaders of the Congress and the Muslim League were silent too. They were busy ushering freedom into the country. That was far more important than rice.

German Mian's elder brother, Anwar Mian, pondered over all this, assuring himself that once azaadi – freedom – had been achieved, prices of rice and all items of daily use would become much cheaper. They might even be available free of cost. The new government would be run by the people of the country.

Anwar Mian spent his afternoons grooming the horses, which were a favorite of his younger brother. He didn't trust the farmhands. The rascals ate up all the jaggery meant for the horses. He personally fed the horses their chickpea. Never mind the oil-cakes and bran, even the grass and the hay could not be accounted for; the scoundrels pilfered everything. A figure lurking outside the front room caught his eye. Who was it? Tentuli's wife, wasn't it? Couldn't the hussy have found a better time to turn up?

'What is it that you want now? Is this any time to visit?'

'I'll come whenever you want me to. There was something I had to say. I'll say it only if you promise not to turn me down.'

'You want money, right? Come at night, I'll give you some.'

The sun hasn't even gone down and the bitch wants money. 'Now that you're asking for money in broad daylight do you plan to return it?'

'No, Mian, I didn't come for money. I was just saying if you'll give me some rice tonight, I'll come and collect it.'

Anwar Mian's face brightened. Laughing, he said, 'Get going, no rice or money for you. Go away now.'

Tentuli's wife knew that this 'no' actually meant 'yes'. Happy, she set off homewards. Anwar Mian called after her, 'Have you heard, Chhoto Bo-Bibi has been released from the labour room. Come in the evenings from tomorrow and massage her legs with oil. And listen, the chhoti ceremony is three days from now. Bring your children for the feast.'

Tentuli's wife acknowledged him, saying, 'Ji,' and resumed walking.

No one from Nani's family would come to the lavish ceremony that was being arranged on the occasion of the birth of her child. Normally the first child was born in the mother's parents' home. The exception in this case was because when Runa's Nana went to his wife's home for the ashtamangala ceremony eight days after the wedding, he swore for some unknown reason never to set foot there again. Nor would he allow his wife to go home. Oddly enough, there had never been any pressure from Nani's family. And no one from either family had ever pleaded with Nana to go. Nani had accepted this without protest. Some had even heard her say that she was far happier here than she had been at home. Although the neighbours had discussed the whole thing threadbare, none of them had dared bring it up in Anwar Mian's house – perhaps because of Anwar Mian's loud voice or his bloodshot eyes.

The arrangements for the six-day ceremony had been flawless. Not even the exorbitant prices in the market could prune the expenses. Several sets of clothes had been bought for the newborn and a number of saris for Nani. Relatives and neighbours had been served a lavish feast and all of them had brought gifts for the newborn. The presents ranged from homemade ghee to a cock, and fruits, all for a glimpse of the child. Only one of them had brought nothing. She was neither a relation nor an in-law of Nani's. She was from Nani's village – her childhood friend, apparently. How had an unmarried woman been allowed to travel on her own ? People gossiped at length about it and cast aspersions on her family for not stopping her from doing so. After all, her house was an hour and a half's walk through the fields.

Later it turned out that she was not there to visit Nani but to meet Mejo Nana. After visiting the newborn, she told Nani, 'Please arrange for me to meet your brother-in-law. Do you remember me telling you about Asgari Begum? The Englishmen arrested Asgari a few days ago. They have burnt her alive. They've also put Hosenara Begum from 24 Parganas in jail. None of the people who went to join the civil disobedience movement have come back. Jamila Khatun has been hanged. But never mind all that, there's no end to it. I'm not here to tell Mejo Mian these stories. He knows everything anyway. I've come to him with a request.'

'Tell me,' said Nani, 'I'll send him a message. Where do you live these days? I know your family has thrown you out. Thank goodness I got married, or my fate would have been the same. Not that I'm particularly happy about it. It's all destiny.'

Nani's friend smiled. 'You've heard of Majera Khatun, haven't you?' she said. 'She has formed a force, which I've joined. You recognized me easily because of the way I'm dressed now. But usually I wear thick pants, strong shoes, a thick coat and a turban to cover my hair. Nobody can tell whether we're men or women. Our financial situation isn't too good and it would be of great help if your brother-in-law could arrange for some money for us.' Nani seemed to have guessed as much already. 'Don't worry,' she said, 'I'm sure we can get you some money. Send someone to me a week from now. I promise you that we will give as much as we can – we'll even sell a few things if we have to.' Reassured of help, the young woman left after lunch.

Meanwhile, the price of rice kept rising. The price of coarse rice had risen from five rupees per mound to fifteen over the past three or four months. Some people were selling their babies for a kilo of rice and men and women were said to be dying of starvation in some places.

Amidst all this, some strange news was heard one day. Traders were transporting rice and lentils by the narrow-gauge railway between Katwa and Ahmedpur when a group of people tried to loot them at Kurmadanga Station. Apparently they had pleaded with the traders for alms before looting them. The traders called in the police, and three or four armed policemen who were on the train chased away a crowd of about a thousand people, beating them up with their sticks. Some had fractured skulls, and others broken arms and legs. But still they didn't let go of their booty. Even the most merciless beating couldn't separate them from what they had looted. It was said that some of them had actually died of the beating and their fingers gripped the sacks like pincers even in death.

The government wasn't taking any steps despite the crisis as everyone was too busy with the war. The newspapers said that the government had fixed the price of rice at five rupees and seventy-five paise, but no one was interested in following the government's orders. The Congress, along with two or three thousand demonstrators, stormed a rice mill in Midnapore, where a large quantity of rice was stashed away. They chanted slogans: 'No hoarding! No exporting!' The five armed guards who were posted at the mill opened fire without a second thought, killing three people and injuring many. About ten protestors were arrested. The government paid no attention to this, nor did they rein in the soaring prices, and the cost of everyday items soared out of control. The people from the Rice Mills' Association openly said that they would not sell their produce at the level fixed by the government. Since they had bought the stuff at high prices they would sell at even higher.

This government had been in place for a long time. Fazlul Haq had become the Prime Minister of Bengal four years ago. People called him Sher-e-Bangla, the Tiger of Bengal. German Mian felt that Haq was a paper tiger who was behaving more like a snake in the grass. Muslim leaders said that Haq Sahib's Krishak Praja Party represented peasants only by name, for actually it was the party of Ashraf Muslims, who claimed foreign ancestry. How would Haq look after the interests of Muslim farmers? He was a puppet controlled by wealthy Hindus. He couldn't sleep at night without bowing and scraping to them. And the Hindus had not only a great deal of money, but also plenty of people to invest in them. From Burrabazar traders to the Tatas and Birlas, everyone was funding the Hindu parties. Had Haq Sahib remained on the side of the Muslims, the Ispahanis would have given the prime minister money for the community in these times of famine and despair. But Haq Sahib had fallen under Shyama Prasad Mukherjee's spell and forgotten the Muslims. And Shyama-babu was the finance minister of Bengal. This clearly showed how easy it was to hoodwink Haq Sahib. That was precisely what Mukherjee had done. Keeping the finance portfolio to himself, he made Haq the prime minister. Khwaja Nizamuddin would have been a far better choice. Besides, Shyama Prasad was not only a member of the Hindu Mahasabha, but he also said nasty things about Muslims everywhere. Haq Sahib pretended not to hear. His own case was complicated. At one point of time he had appeared to be a representative of the Muslim League, and it had seemed that his Krishak Praja Party might merge with the League. But it was different now. His activities in cahoots with the Hindu Mahasabha had marked him out as nothing but a pimp seeking power. He had done nothing for the qaum, barring his friends and relatives. He had begun consorting with the Hindus at a time when all of Bengal's Muslims were starving, and had handed over the larder keys to Shyama Prasad, who was a sworn enemy of Muslims. While Muslims lay in their beds trying to quieten their growling stomachs, Shyama-babu was holding Hindu Mahasabha processions, badmouthing Muslims to his heart's content. Just a few months ago he had announced at the top of his voice at a public gathering, 'Let the Muslims pack their bags and leave India.'

Why should they? Was India his ancestral property? German Mian felt a writhing anger.

Runa's Nani emerged from the labour-room after forty days. She had a habit of writing down all that was on her mind in a notebook. However, for two or three months now, she had written nothing. Now, Kamrunnesa began writing afresh, in the manner of a diary – though her words were mostly misspelt. But there was no continuity. For the most part, the things she had heard found their place, scattered and unconnected, in a notebook covered in green paper.

On the first day Kamrunnesa wrote:

I have had a beautiful daughter. I had meant to call her

Lakshmi, but he didn't agree. Maulana Sahib has named her Zahura. It is a wonderful name. Lakshmi would not have been a bad nickname for her. He said, since there is great poverty everywhere, to name her after the goddess of wealth in these times would be unjust to people. There is strife all over the world.

When I was at my parents', I heard stories about how Lakshmi turned into rice grains to save people from starving. When a poor cowherd was sobbing from hunger, Lakshmi gave her rice seeds. The color of that rice was like gold, and it was fragrant. I am reminded of this story whenever I smell the aroma of Bhimshal rice. The old woman who worked at my parents' house used to say that Lakshmi gave people just a small quantity of rice seeds – but that was enough to have the grains growing everywhere. The hills, the ponds, the canals, the fields all overflowed with the crop.

I have been eating Bhootmuri rice these past forty days. It is said that this rice boosts the flow of breast milk. Before my sister left our parents' house, she used to eat Kabirajshal rice. These people have no Kabirajshal rice. It was available at my parents' house.

Dozens of people come to this house for their meals every day. I'm not inclined to turn so many people down. Mejo Bhaijan measures out the rice these days. I don't know how all these people will manage. Rice, potato and sugar are hard to get. We have enough rice for a year at home, but how can you eat rice alone? Mejo Bhaijan has bought a mound of potatoes. I do not know how long it will last in this huge family. But then it is not supposed to be my concern. Mejo Bhabi will worry about it. Still, if you are part of a household you have to think of these things. You have to think of the villagers too. For a fistful of rice they're selling the animals that helped plough their fields. People are dying every day. The price of rice has risen to thirty rupees a mound. Babies are being sold in Burdwan and Nadia districts. When I look at my Lakshmi, these things make me tremble. They're selling children for five to twenty rupees. But then who will buy them? Who has the money to support a child?

It seems a girl was sold in exchange for a mound and a half of rice in Birbhum. Unable to feed his wife and child, a Muslim weaver jumped into the Kansai river and drowned. His wife threw their younger child into the river. She was in the process of burying the elder child when a lower-caste Hindu rescued him.

My friend had come. She stayed for three days. He objected, but Mejo Bhaijan said she could stay as long as she liked. A couple of stories she told me made me lose my appetite at dinner. She told me how a woman and her mother from Agartala village under Nandigram police station in Midnapur were widowed in a tornado. The rest of the family had drowned. The starving mother and daughter began to beg, and went all the way to Kakdwip. An accountant there offered them shelter. He gave them a room to stay in, and he assaulted the daughter repeatedly. Not content with being the only one, he got others to assault her too. The evil accountant has set up a factory for her. The devil and his friends assaulted a Muslim woman the same way when she went to Kakdwip from Khulna. He and his friends used the woman for their own enjoyment and gave her father a small plot of land and ordered him to remain silent about the goings-on. They even threatened to kill the family if it was revealed the family was Muslim. My friend and her group visited them secretly. The woman said, 'I have no family, what will I do with honour? My stomach is empty, what good will it do keeping it covered?'

Meanwhile, Netaji has left India. From his voice on the radio we know he's alive. People from the city are moving to the villages because vegetables are cheaper here and now there is a shortage of vegetables here too. The Quit India movement started a few days later. He was saying he would join the movement but abandoned his plans after a scolding from Mejo Bhaijan. Maulana Azad has been jailed. My friend was here again. This time too she came for money. She needs the money because Maulana's wife is in trouble. She needs help. The Maulana could never provide much money to his family. On top of that he has been jailed for a year. Maulana's wife Zulekha Begum, however, has no regrets about it. She has sent a letter to Bapuji saying that she had not expected her man to be jailed for a year – his exploits should have fetched him a longer term in jail – and that she would take charge of the Khilafat Committee in Bengal in her husband's absence. Zulekha Begum needed funds, and so my friend was going about raising money.

He said, Shyama-babu has parted ways with Haq Sahib as the government is not dispatching food to Midnapore. Haq Sahib's throne is tottering too. The League is not happy with him. The Lieutenant Governor cannot stand his speeches either.

A few days later I heard Nawab Nazimuddin had got the throne. Suhrawardy was the food minister now. People thought they would get food at last, but their sufferings increased. They kept dropping dead like flies. Tentuli the farmhand said corpses could be seen in the bushes. Jackals, dogs, vultures and hawks had no lack of food now. The ponds were dry; no water could be had at the mosque either. Water had to be fetched from distant places. The League had opened community kitchens in many places to provide free food. They had plenty of money. The Ispahanis gave them both food and cash. Ramlochan the Kaviraj said the Ispahanis had apparently bought all the rice at a high price and were hoarding it. People weren't even strong enough to walk to the free kitchens. The leaves on the trees had wilted; those were not edible any more. Fuel was available but what could people cook? They died eating the hyacinth from ponds whose waters were highly stale and polluted. Mejo Bhaijan told us a story about an old man from Ujjalpur who was returning home after failing to get any food. He tripped on the raised land between two fields and fell down by the canal. Three jackals tore into him and ate him alive.

Lakshmi, that is Zahura, turned four. Kamrunnesa, Runa's Nani, was in the family way again, and Runa's Nana began to dream once more. But Nana had changed a great deal during these years. He no longer had bitter arguments with the Maulana. On the contrary, their viewpoints now converged in many respects. Nana continued to dream and to weave different versions of his dreams.

The time for Zahura's Bismillah Khani, the day she would start learning to write, was fast approaching. It had to be done when she was four years, four months and four days old, though given the state of the nation elaborate ceremonies had all but vanished from people's lives. German Mian had another dream on the night of the Bismillakhani. Maulana Sahib had performed the ceremonies and spent the entire day at their house. They chatted at length and he left late in the afternoon. In the evening, German Mian surmised that dreams would not spare him that night, so he had an early dinner and went to sleep. That night, he dreamt that an elderly man was approaching him, holding a sword in one hand and a rosary in the other. He was riding a four-legged creature. Is this the apocalypse, wondered German Mian. Terrified, he began to flee, but in his dream his feet moved painfully slowly. The elderly man followed him. Suddenly, German Mian saw a mosque looming ahead of him and he ran inside for shelter. It was so teeming with people that he could not even get a toehold. Most of those present were like skeletons, dressed in tattered clothes. German Mian had not performed his wuzu, his ablutions. There was no water to be found anywhere. He was dying of thirst. His throat was parched. But the water from the taps was toxic, undrinkable. Suddenly he saw a mound of earth behind the mosque, running his hands over it, he attempted the Tayammum or dry ablutions. The moment he touched the mound, three birds flew out of it. They were alien birds. Were these the Ababil birds who had stoned to death the soldiers on elephant-back? The three birds began conversing among themselves. German Mian felt certain they did not belong to this world. They were shaped like distorted maps. Taking off their clothes, they began to bathe in blood and appeared to transform gradually into humans. Humans, women. The ground was splattered with blood. German Mian knew that the clothes contained the beating hearts of the three bewitching women. He escaped unobserved with their clothes. After bathing, when they couldn't find their clothes anywhere, German Mian revealed himself to them. He told them he would return their clothes on one condition. He wanted one of them to carry him on their wings to his destination. The smallest of the three birds agreed and asked 'Where do you want to go, huzoor?' German Mian could not decide on his destination – Persia or the deserts of Arabia? Then he said he would go to Pakistan, east Pakistan. The bird chuckled. While airborne, German Mian made up his mind to become a member of the League that very day. Never mind the Maulana! He wanted to live in this dream. Considering how his dreams were being shattered every day, retaining his sense of reality during a dream or in a semi-wakeful state would cause his dreams too yield to him easily. They would escape him despite being within touching distance.

That night he clearly saw a beautiful, unmarried woman. She was wandering about on an uncultivated plot of land where crops had never grown. German Mian walked across this plot of land and came to a cross-road. Numerous other roads met at this point – winding roads that could be mistaken for snakes. He realized that dreadful battles had broken out on every street leading off this gigantic junction. Most of the land and people of the world were being destroyed. Only a few would survive and he was one of them. In his dream he had no idea whether his wife, child or any of his relations were alive. Night had descended on the planet and a few scattered stars twinkled in the sky. Suddenly he saw an elderly man dressed in a white pirhan approaching him.

German Mian felt alert and ready. He realized he would become a participant in this partition, a process of endless partition, which could not be stopped. He rose from his bed for a drink of water to soothe his parched throat and thought about how the water here had a very bad taste. It was then that he decided to move to Pakistan.

The next morning German Mian felt ill. He could no longer suppress the story of his dream of the previous night. No sooner did the saga of the dream become known than there was mayhem at home. German Mian's elder brother decided to take him to Shah Rustam's shrine in Salar. Mejo Mian had heard his Burra Abba, his father's grandfather say that Khwaja Mohammad Sharif was the thirteenth descendant of Hazrat Abu Bakr, the first Caliph of Islam – his son Shah Rustam came to India from Khorasan several years ago. This extremely erudite man finally settled in Salar in Murshidabad. He received a great deal of land as gift from King Shah Alam. His grave was in Salar. However, instead of following in his footsteps, his son Serajuddin took the post of principal Qazi at Gaur. Sultan Ghiasuddin was very fond of him. His son Shah Azizullah busied himself with religious matters, and returned to Salar. Mufti Mohammad Moyez was a member of this family, the bosom friend and tutor of Prince Humayun Zah. Moyez Sahib eventually had to serve the English. Although Khondkar Obaidul Akbar and his son Fazle Rabbi worked for the nawab, they were learned men too. But as the saying goes, Allahtaala takes away family glory after a few generations. Their progeny were now in that situation. Everyone was exploiting Shah Rustam to survive. But Rustam's shrine was exceptionally potent, and unless German Mian was taken there his fate would always hold nightmares for him. Accordingly, an awning was strung up on an ox-cart and a thick mattress was laid out on it. German Mian was a man of luxury, so it was decided that a radio would also be taken along. If they left very early in the morning, they would reach Salar in four hours. A lantern was hung beneath the cart to dispel the darkness of the night. Tentuli was at the helm, steering the ox cart.

As they were passing Palsha on their way to Daskamalgram, they saw a strange sight. A body lay in front of a primary school made of earth, with a thatched roof. The face wasn't clear in the half darkness, but German Mian had no doubt it was a woman's body. Tentuli was asked to turn the cart around. 'No, we cannot go back,' declared Mejo Mian. 'Drive straight to Salar, Tentuli.' German Mian was not accustomed to defying his elder brother. Half-sitting, half-lying under the awning, he busied himself with reconstructing the face of the corpse. In his head he recited the Ayatul Kursi, the throne verse of the Quran which emphasized Allah's power over the universe. This would make the devil flee from his presence. He also knew that there was no alternative to the Ayatul Kursi to rid himself of the agony of leaving the safe haven of his home, his Al-makam-al-amin that was tearing his heart apart. Even as he reconstructed the face, he recited softly,

'Allah is the immortal eternal entity who holds the entire world firmly in his grip. There is no god but him. He does not sleep and slumber cannot touch him. Everything on earth and in the sky belongs to him. No one can make a recommendation in his court without his permission. He knows all that is known to man, and all that is unknown to man is not unknown to him. What he knows lies beyond the limits of human knowledge.

It is a different matter if he wishes to teach any of this to mankind. His kingdom encompasses the earth and the sky. Looking after all this does not exhaust him. In truth he is a noble entity, the finest.'

German Mian fell asleep reciting the Ayatul Kursi and reconstructing the face of the dead woman. When you go to sleep after reading this verse, Allah sends an angel your way. The angel would guard German Mian until he woke up. Therefore, there were six creatures on or near the cart now – Anwar Mian, German Mian, Tentuli, the angel, and two black oxen. The last two were only slightly visible in the dark and Tentuli kept up the occasional banter with them. Anwar Mian wondered about the woman. Who had killed her and left her here? How would she be buried? Inna lillahe wa inna elaihe rajeoon.We belongs to Allah and to him we shall return.

Only the angel put all thoughts aside and accompanied the cart like a guard, sometimes perched on the awning, sometimes whirling around the lantern beneath the cart. Not even daybreak brought him relief – he would be done only when German Mian awoke. But this young angel knew that German Mian's wakefulness was actually another kind of sleep. Just as fate never did hold dreamless sleep for German Mian, he too never entirely left the world of sleep and descended to the real world. Would the angel then have to stay with German Mian till he sank into eternal sleep? He didn't know. He had no task other than to follow orders. But he quite liked this tall man whom he visited frequently. Although his visits were professional he had his likes and dislikes, even if he wasn't allowed to express them. The young angel decided to sneak into German Mian's sleep for a glimpse of the world of his dreams. He discovered that this man's soul was housed in a place just like Dar-ul-makam, or Home. Offering a mental sajdah to Allahtaala, prostrating himself in his head before Allah, he said: 'To the one who has made room for us to dwell in his infinite compassion, where there is neither suffering nor fatigue, to Allah I proffer my sajdah.'

~ Dar-ul-Makam ~

HOME

Mejo Mian had draped his dhoti around himself in the ceremonial style. The Khadim of Shah Rustam's shrine was displeased at this. What sort of Hindu behavior was on display here? Without voicing his objections, he simply ordered Mejo Mian to take the dhoti off and drape it like a lungi. Then he proceeded to brief the gathering on why Muslims should fight for India. German Mian realized at once that this man was a Deobandi, a member of the Deoband, the revivalist movement in Sunni Islam founded by Mohammad Kasem and Maulana Rashid. But no Deobandi ever became a Khadim, who headed services at shrines – how had this man come to occupy the post? They were forbidden from worshipping at shrines or paying obeisance to pirs – the only entity they bowed to was Allahtaala himself. He listened to the Khadim's Hidayat, his guidance, with close attention.

'What does our sacred faith of Islam mean, brothers? It means peace. We want peace. If we were to instigate discord and dispute at a time our people are in peril, Khudataala will never forgive us. The first person whom the holy lord created and sent into the world was Hazrat Adam Safi, peace be upon him. To which land was he sent? None other than this one, to sacred India. Thus the world began with India. Madni Sahib, our dearest brother Alam Husain Ahmad Madni, has told us that all the Muslims in Hindustan consider India their original home. Why talk of Muslims alone – all the races everywhere in the world originate from Hindustan. Allahbarkataala has sent prophets to many different lands. Why has he done so? Because when those lands are sunk in ignorance, when people fight and kill one another, these prophets arrive to provide guidance. They move humans from the path of evil to that of good. India was not deprived of the lord's blessings either. Another learned brother of ours, Maulana Mohammad Mian has referred to a set of instructions from the book *Our Hindustan and Its Virtues*, which states that the Muslim race is compelled to love and serve Hindustan – that is what the sacred faith of Islam teaches us. Allah has given special importance to India. So we have to come forward to work for this country. All of you have heard of Ghulam Azad Bilgrami. He also concurs with this. Maulana Mian said Allah's first creation was named Noor-e-Mohammadi – the light of Mohammad. This light was first gifted to Hazrat Adam. Then it was given in turn to the other prophets. The last person that it reached was Mohammad Rasulullah. In other words brothers, the light of Mohammad, peace be upon him, was born on the soil of India.'

Everyone said, 'Alhamdulillah, praise be to the lord.'

'My brothers, in Islam, Mecca, Medina and Jerusalem are Allahtaala's favourite places. This Hindustan of ours is also the land of mercy for Khudataala. Hazrat Ali Rahamatullah had said that the lord sent Adam Safi to Seren Dweep first. Where is this Seren Dweep? In India, my brothers. Those who are dreaming today of splitting this land are not walking the path of Allah. The first woman, Bibi Hawwa, was kept in Jeddah after being created. There was Seren Dweep on one side and Jeddah on the other. Our original parents met for the first time near Mecca. Adam, peace be upon him, built the Kaa'aba there, and then returned to India with Hawwa Bibi. There were neither trains nor buses those days, or even planes. How they must have suffered, travelling on foot. Had they not walked all that way, how do you suppose there would be humans on earth? It was all Allahtaala's will. Say with me, Subhanallah, Glory be to Allah.'

Trying to match his voice with the others as they chanted 'Subhanallah', German Mian gulped. Was this really the Salar that he had wanted to come to? He had had a different picture of the village in his head. He had assumed that all the Muslims here were fighting in favour of Pakistan, that they had declared a holy war against the infidels. Had his weakness for the Muslim League made his elder brother send him here, so that he could also repose his faith in the Congress? German Mian didn't know where his brother had vanished, but he was feeling quite tired. The long journey on the bullock cart had taken its toll, even though he had slept most of the way. That was his way of escaping his thoughts about the corpse he had seen. Nothing could be compared with sleep. Those who could not bring themselves to love sleep would never fathom the mystery of death. Had the corpse been buried properly? He had not been able to participate in the funeral prayer, and yet the janaza was their collective responsibility – not discharging it could mean perilous danger. His heart grew remorseful, but what could he possibly do now? A man appeared and escorted him out of the shrine. 'Arrangements have been made for your stay nearby, huzoor. Come with me. You must be exhausted. The house I'm taking you to belongs to a friend of your brother's. Your brother has left for his own home.' German Mian was a little surprised. Had his brother gone back in a hurry without telling him because he wanted to conduct the burial of that woman? He followed the man without speaking.

The house where arrangements had been made for German Mian's stay was ten minutes' walk from the shrine, and from its front room, in the evening, the night sky was visible. German Mian became wistful whenever he looked at the sky. A strange fear seemed to suffocate him, and yet he could not stop himself from looking upwards. Although the star-studded sky of Salar raised a storm of terror in his heart, he continued gazing at the beautiful form of this extraordinary world created by the Almighty. Suddenly, a booming voice floated in from the unknown. 'Are you afraid, Mian?' German Mian could see no one in the sky, but when he lowered his eyes he discovered a figure in a white pirhan standing in front of him. 'Don't be afraid. My name is Zulfiqar Mian. I am your brother's friend. We used to be business partners once upon a time, dealing in jaggery.'

The name was familiar. All he knew was that arrangements had been made for him to stay at the house of a friend of his brother's. Although he was somewhat reassured on hearing Zulfiqar Mian's name, his fear was not entirely dispelled. This was partly on account of viewing the night sky, and partly the effect of the baritone that had dropped from the above. Still under the impact of this fear, German Mian was not able to speak, but Zulfiqar continued to converse with his guest. This man did not know how to stop talking. Khudataala had made some people in this fashion – their tongues, like galloping horses, were incapable of pausing.

'My grandfather had told me a story, a chilling story. Not that you will be afraid – it will actually amuse you. My grandfather heard it from his grandfather. His forefathers came from Turkey. We had a traditional business of selling horses. From horses to jaggery – only the lord we worship knows what a man's destiny holds for him. But forget about that, Janab-e-Mianbhai.'

German Mian had no idea when he had recalled all this, that he was now being told to forget it. But he said nothing. Zulfiqar Mian did not pause.

'Do you know the name of the star you see there in the Qibla sky that points towards Mecca?'

Although German Mian could indeed see the evening star

in the western sky, he did not respond. Zulfiqar Mian was not really asking him a question at all. This was how he spoke, like a schoolmaster.

'Its name is Al Zohra.'

German Mian was reminded of his daughter. So his daughter was named after the evening star. Magnificent! He had no idea. He began to develop a fondness for Zulfiqar Mian.

'You will see the same star in the east at dawn. In between, a variety of twinkling stars will move across the sky all night. That beautiful sight of the heavens will make your head reel. And this is just one sky there are six more. If just one of them is so beautiful, can you imagine what the other six must be like? If you cannot sleep, lie back quietly in your bullock-cart and look at the sky – you'll realize how powerful Allahtaala is, how much effort he has put into creating this universe.'

German Mian finally spoke 'you were talking of a frightening story, weren't you? Tell me the story. I will listen while gazing at the sky.'

Zulfiqar Mian smiled, and then turned grave. No smile in the world lasts very long.

He began to weave his horror story on a sombre vein.

'A long time ago, a widow lived with her son. One day she told him, shut the door son, I'm afraid. Her son was astonished, for he did not know what fear was. When he asked his mother, she said, fear is terror. So the boy left home to look for fear. He knew that fear did not wait outside the door to be let in like a guest; it would lurk in a forest or in ocean waves. He kept walking, asking everyone he met, but no one could inform him of the whereabouts of fear. Finally he arrived close to a mountain, where there were forty dacoits, desert bandits sporting long beards and dressed like Bedouins. The very sight of them was enough to make one faint. Exhausted, the young man sat down near them. This scared the dacoits. One of them summoned enough courage to ask, where have you come from, boy? Don't you know birds are afraid to come here, and even insects scurry away when they see us? Here are our swords, we are ruthless, come near us and we'll slice your head off. The young man was not frightened in the least. "I am looking for fear," he said. "Do you know where I can find it?"

"'Fear is wherever we are," answered the bandit.

"'Where?" asked the young man.

"'There in that graveyard. Go and take a look. Light a fire there and make some halwa for us – take along all you need. When you bring the halwa, I'll answer your question."

"'The young man went off to the graveyard to make the halwa. When the aroma began to waft across the graves, an arm emerged from one of them, and a nasal voice demanded, "Give me some halwa." Rather amused, the young man said "Of course I'll give you some. People don't get halwa even when they're alive, and this corpse has such high hopes. Stretch out your arm." As soon as the arm was extended the young man scalded it with the spatula with which he had been cooking. At once the arm disappeared. The young man took the halwa to the bandits, who were astonished. How would they frighten someone who wasn't even afraid of the graveyard? After much discussion, they sent him off to a haunted house, which was occupied by all sorts of vicious spirits, jinns and nymphs. But these beings could not frighten him either. The dacoits sent him to all the places that people were afraid to visit, but none could scare him. Yet, his mother wasn't someone to lie. Fear was bound to be lurking somewhere, waiting in hiding, which was why he couldn't find it. He would not return home till he had found fear. As the young man pondered over all this in a garden, he noticed three birds. They dipped their bodies into the pond in the garden and instantly turned into houris, those enchanting virgin companions of the faithful in Paradise.'

German Hosain interrupted Zulfiqar Ali's story. He had dreamt of three birds turning into houris, he said, but in his dream the birds had bathed not in water but in blood.

Zulfiqar Mian returned to his story, ignoring the interlude.

'After the bath the three houris sat down to eat. Before they began sipping from their bowls, one of them extended her arm towards the young man. What arm? It was the same scalded, colourless one that had emerged from the grave, asking for halwa. The arm said, "I'll drink your blood from this bowl today." The young man chuckled. It seemed to him that the arm was growing longer, and had acquired a pair of eyes, a nose, teeth, two ears, and nails. The houri's arm was dead, and yet it kept growing.'

This frightened German Mian. 'For heavens sake, stop now,

Zulfiqar Bhai. I don't want to hear this story anymore. Aren't you going to show me the night sky? I'm very hungry.'

Zulfiqar Mian stopped his story and asked for dinner to be served. A woven mat of palm fronds was spread out on the ground, and a feast set out on it. There was rice, fried aubergine, and beef curried red, the sight of which made German Mian salivate. Nowhere else in Bengal could one get beef curry as delicious as in Salar, he reminded himself. At least twenty cows were slaughtered in this village every day. People from neighbouring villages came here to buy the meat. He ate his beef and rice with great relish, after which he read the Tahajjud namaz.

The Tirmizi Hadith says that the Tahajjud namaz not only washes off a person's sins, it also keeps him from committing more in the future. After the namaz they went out on the veranda of the front room and climbed down the stairs to the front yard. A bullock-cart without any awning stood there. Sitting on it, they lit their bidis – Maqid's bidis, tied with red threads, were far superior to cigarettes. Those who had not tasted Salar's beef and bidis had missed a lot in their lives. German Mian sometimes felt he could leave his village and live here just for these two things and if Pakistan was formed with Salar being a part of it, nothing would be better. He knew this district would never remain with Hindustan, no matter how much the Khadim at Shah Rustam's shrine shouted. Most of the local leaders had already said as much. But there was a well-known person here, Zakaria Sahib, who had even been the mayor of Calcutta, who was speaking up for the Congress. Anyway a few loud voices would never be able to stop Pakistan in its tracks. If Pakistan was formed, Murshidabad and Malda were certain to be included in it. Why not buy some land, build a house and stay on here in Salar well in advance? He could live a life of comfort, eating his beef and smoking his bidis. Even if his dreams disappeared with the smoke from the bidis, they would remain like the fragrance of the tobacco in his lungs, in the gaps between his teeth.

'See that star there, Mian? Can you identify it? Do you know its name?' Zulfiqar Mian asked, pointing to a corner of the sky.

'The Dog Star. Sirius.'

'Those names mean nothing! That star is known as the Ash-Shi'ra. The sacred lord has described a sura about stars in the Quran – the An-Najm. That's where it says, waannahu huwa rabbu sa-Shi'ra – it is he who is the lord of the star Shira.'

'The dog in Sirius. I was told as a child that the diseases of dogs are caused by this star. As a dog in our neighbourhood was about to give birth...' German Mian started to speak, but Zulfiqar Sahib butted in 'Stop all these anti-Sharia practices of yours, Mian. Don't pay attention to the infidels. As a Muslim you cannot believe such things. Shira is twenty times more powerful than the sun, it is the brightest star in the night sky and its god is Khudataala himself – waannahu huwa rabbu sa-Shi'ra – he is the owner of your Sirius. The Hadith Sharif says that the sacred lord created these stars in order to decorate

Paradise, to drive away the devils, and to light the way for humans and his other creations in the darkness. This star will be Pakistan's flag, for it is etched on the breast of every Muslim in the world.'

'That dog in our neighbourhood died, you know, and the star was not part of the constellation that night. Believe me!'

'Enough, Mian. Don't keep talking of dogs. Nara-e-Takbir, Allahu Akbar. Say it out loud, God is great.'

German Mian subsided, for although he believed in astrology, he did not have the courage to assert himself boldly before Zulfiqar Sahib; besides, silence was preferable. He often had to retreat this way. A few days before he arrived here, he had been reading Haji Mohammad Zardar Khan's book, *The Edicts of the Lord*, with great attention. It contained diagrams for everything from hypnotising people to getting rid of troubles. Although each of those diagrams floated in front of German Mian's eyes, the beauty of the sky prevented him from gathering the courage to talk about them. In the glow of the Dog Star, he was reminded of another extraordinary drawing. Resembling a scarecrow, it had Arabic letters inscribed on its chest, like patterns on a pirhan. If a person's friendship was being sought, these letters would have to be written with great care in the twelve squares on the chest of the scarecrow sketch and the whole thing would have to be buried beneath the veranda of the room belonging to the person concerned.. When the person walked across this grave of the scarecrow, his or her mind would undergo a transformation. Proper application would ensure that, by God's grace, even a lifelong enemy could turn into a friend in an instant. How about burying that scarecrow in the veranda of Hindustan and Pakistan? Why was he indulging in these mad thoughts! Were they, those seeking partition, people who lived in houses? And if they didn't, how would there be verandas? German Mian's penchant for bizarre thoughts refused to leave him when Zulfiqar Sahib made him snap out of his reverie. 'Do you know the name of the star near the left foot of what you refer to as Kalpurush?' Without waiting for a response, he continued, 'That's the Arhijal – I don't know what the Hindus call it. Do you know the Nakhoda? Allahtaala has created this star for the convenience of seamen. When they sail, they use this star to set their course. There are so many thousands of stars, Mian, do you suppose I know all of them? The Almighty has created such a wonderful world, his abilities are unbounded, he is the most merciful of all the merciful. Come, our stargazing is done for the day. Go to bed quickly – sleep does not come easily in an unfamiliar place.'German Mian rose to his feet. He was to sleep in the front room. After Zulfiqar Mian had disappeared inside the house, he lay back in his bed. His dreams seemed to have been lying in wait for him. No sooner did slumber descend on him than all of them came rushing up. In his dreams German Mian was no longer a human, but was instead turning into a snail. His pace and rhythm were slow, his hard body rolling gently across land or water. And with that body he sensed the presence of a corpse which he had left behind in his own village. In his dream the body of the dead woman lengthened, and German Mian in the form of a snail looked for a wound on it. The throat would have turned blue had she been throttled, while if she had been battered to death it would have left a reddish mark. But since there are no colours in dreams besides black and white, and since the snail has no more than two senses, it could not experience anything but the touch of the corpse and the indescribable taste of death. German Mian sorely missed the remaining senses in his dream. If he had even been a bee, he would have been able to see the disfigured face of the dead woman, which had rotted by now. He climbed up the dead body in the form of a snail, realising that this corpse was in fact the entire world, which a snail could not hope to traverse completely. And yet it was this impossible task that he had been forced to embark on. Just like sleep, dreams too have several levels. Moving up and down between these stages and levels, like a game of snakes and ladders, exhausted German Mian. And in the midst of all this, the dreamer felt thirsty. About to pick up the glass of water near his head in his semi-wakeful state, he discovered that what his hand had touched was soft, warm and fluffy. It could have been a furry creature. But his hand was scorched when he tried to grasp it. German Mian groaned as the furry creature cried 'Miaow' and retreated to a distance. At once a blue glow flashed across the room. He had never seen such a strange light in his life. It took not just the eyes but the entire body into a world without boundaries, and the source of the beams was a pair of eyes belonging to a four-legged creature resembling a cat. The sight of this mysterious beast multiplied his thirst a hundredfold. He searched again for his jug of water. Seeing this, the peculiar cat now spoke in a human voice. 'There's no water Mian, I've used it up for my wuzu. I have to read the namaz at dawn, there isn't long to go.'

German Mian's limbs were paralysed. He felt he could not speak but still he tried his utmost to make a sound with his vocal cords. Inarticulately he groaned, 'Wu...zu!' It was not evident whether the animal heard him. But then German Mian did not know whether this creature from a different world might have used a different sense organ to understand what he had said. It began to speak, in Hindi.

'I am Jul, the badshah of jinns. I have a plea to make of you, lord of the world.'

'Plea?'

'I shall tell you later. But first allow me to inform you that my name is Jul Jenahen. King Sulaiman has killed my son Beelzebul. He was a loveable child and naughty too. He left behind a daughter named Lucifa. She was married to the king of Babel, but they were divorced. A girl with no father but very beautiful. It is my desire that you marry her.'

German Mian seemed to find some similarities between Lucifa and another woman whom he knew. But she was human, made of earth. And Lucifa was a woman of fire. He also knew that marriage between jinns and humans was illegitimate. If earth and fire came together, earth would be burnt to ashes.

The elders had forbidden the burning of the earth. That was why crippled people were summoned to light the fires at brick kilns. Their acts were not considered sins. A marriage between a jinn and a human would not bring forth children. He did not say anything openly to badshah Jul – partly because his vocal cords were paralysed, but more because German Mian did not want to antagonize the king of jinns. Although humans were born superior to jinns, they could not do a quarter of all that jinns were capable of. jinns could take on any form at any time, and turn invisible if they wanted to. They could travel faster than the wind. jinns also read the minds of humans very easily. Was the jinn reading German Mian's mind too? That could mean trouble. Jul Jenahen continued speaking to German Mian. 'Listen to me, my son. King Solaiman told me, he put his hand on my heart and told me, your knowledge has opened forty-nine doors. Trusting this knowledge I am telling you, you may be married, but that is not a problem for me.'

German Mian realized that a severe crisis was upon him. He could feel the absence of Kamrunnesa, Zahura's mother, in his bones. Finding him alone, a married man, the badshah of jinns was trying to make him go astray. Even in his semi-wakeful state, he felt very bad about it. A phrase from the real world saved him this time – 'the namaz is better than sleep'. The azaan of dawn could be heard. He had to get out of bed, but his body seemed to be revolting. Sleep was determined to keep him in his bed. Caught in the dilemma of whether to arise or not, he tossed and turned, but Zulfiqar Mian's powerful voice made him jump up. 'Come on Mian, let us read the namaz. I don't go to the mosque, I do it at home.' German Mian was accustomed to visiting the mosque, though. The reward of reading the namaz at the mosque was seventy times more. Alevi Muslims did not usually go to the mosque – they didn't care to. German Mian was quite surprised to see that even though Zulfiqar Mian accepted all the practices followed in this country, he had not given up on this one. He would have to give Zulfiqar Mian a piece of his mind one of these days. The mosque was the lord's home – why should he not visit it? After all, they read the namaz to gain Allahtaala's compassion. But then all this could be discussed later. For now he needed to clarify the matter of Jul Junahen, the badshah of jinns. Did Zulfiqar Mian harbour jinns at home? Or was the house not protected with an amulet? Who knew? German Mian got out of bed for his ablutions. Starting with a visit to the toilet, istenja, going on to meswak(brushing his teeth) with a neem branch, and finally the wuzu. Using a prayer mat, and going through the two rakats, rituals of movements and words of the dawn prayers he turned to offer his obeisance to God. 'O sacred lord, save me from the menace of this jinn. You are all powerful, all compassionate, protect me from this threat.'

Folding the mat, German Mian restrained himself from discussing the previous night's dream even though he had intended to. The account of a slow-moving creature in the form of a snail witnessing a constantly expanding corpse might lead Zulfiqar Ali to suspect insanity. Therefore he brought up the subject of jinns, which did not fall in the purview of his strange dream. Hearing of the badshah of jinns, the head of the household was furious. 'What do you mean!' he bellowed. 'A jinn in my house? And that too a Shah!' Zulfiqar Mian had long harboured a weakness for his own name. Hazrat Ali's sword was named Zulfiqar – both its edges were razor sharp. Reminded of this again, he thought to himself, Ali's scimitar would redden this land; he was determined to slay the jinn in feline form. But catching a glimpse of this jinn by daylight was well-nigh impossible. To cover this shortcoming, he began to rattle off stories about his ancestors. 'You know, Bhaijan, one of my forefathers came to India during the era of Ikhtiyar ad-Din Mohammad Bin Bakhtiar Khilji. I don't know exactly which generation of my ancestors was one of those seventeen horsemen, but he was among them. Even the badshah of Bengal had escaped through the back door on hearing the hoof beats of Arab stallions. And this is a mere jinn. Don't worry Mian, I will teach him such a lesson that leave alone Salar, he will flee from Bengal, Bihar and Orissa, and won't know where to hide. But it seems to me that Bhabi Sahiba must be fetched. You cannot live alone here anymore.'

When German Mian didn't respond, Zulfiqar Mian proceeded to air all that he knew about jinns.

'We mustn't leave it till too late. To subjugate a jinn, he must first be brought under control. This needs courage, strength and patience. It's of no use otherwise. An attack by jinns could even lead to death. But the lord is our protector;

whatever he wills will take place. You, Mian, will have to be more devoted and engage yourself in meditating on the lord. To fulfil your objectives, you must light incense sticks late at night, sprinkle rose-ittar on yourself, read the Ayatul Kursi and draw a circle around yourself. Sitting inside it, you must read this a hundred times:

'Qalat ya ayyuhal mala u inni ulqiya ilayya kitabun karim Innahu min Sulaimana wa innahu bismil lahir rahmanir Rahim.'He said, 'A letter worthy of respect has been delivered to me. It is from Solomon and is as follows: "In the name of Allah, most gracious, most merciful…"'

Not enjoying the conversation with Zulfiqar Mian any longer, German Mian decided to visit Rustam's shrine. He displayed a sense of urgency about this, practically ordering that a message be sent to his brother Anwar Husain for Zahura's mother to be sent to Salar quickly. He considered whether his wife could live in the front room of Zulfiqar Ali's house – if that would even be proper. If not, they would have to look for a house. He did not hesitate in mentioning this to Zulfiqar Mian. Zulfiqar Ali said, as though obeying German Mian's orders, 'Everything will be taken care of. You've barely been here a couple of days. Don't be impatient. You are my friend's brother. Besides, Anwar Bhai has helped me a great deal. I will certainly do my bit for his brother.' Waving his hands like problem-solving magic wands, Zulfiqar Ali went into the inner rooms to arrange for breakfast.

It took quite some time for him to reach Shah Rustam's

shrine. The sunlight was glaring. German Mian was fond of luxuries and he grew tired rather quickly. Zulfiqar Mian was impassive. He was small in build, but had long arms and looked just like a Turk. There was also something a little Greek and a little Iranian about him. He reminded one of Kemal Pasha – the only thing missing was the cigarette dangling from his lips. Even with long strides it was difficult to keep pace with him.

Pir Sahib was seated in a room next to the shrine, surrounded by countless disciples and students. When he saw them enter he said, 'Welcome, my friends.' Then he addressed Zulfiqar Ali. 'This is your friend's brother, isn't he?' Nodding, they sat down before him. Zulfiqar Ali whispered something to Pir Sahib, who roared, 'What? Jul has taken shelter in your house? How dare he? And calling himself a badshah! I'd put him in a bottle and tossed him into the river, this time I'll have to toss him into the ocean. He must have freed himself somehow and is back to these devilish ways.'

Pir Sahib proceeded to address his disciples. 'Do you see, my brothers? The plight of the world? Do you know who the ancestors of these jinns are? Just as Hazrat Adam, peace be upon him, is ours, their first one was Al Jan. He was a genuine jinn, spending his days in devotion and prayer to Allah. Just as evil has percolated into humans, many jinns too no longer follow the way of the lord; they are travelling on the path of sin. Jul Menahin lives in human beings' houses now. That too, the front rooms of honest people. These jinns are called Aamir. They enjoy the homes of human beings. Another variety of jinns revel in conversing with children, they are known as Aarwa. jinns can be devils too. But the jinn that can beat the devil at his own game is known as Maarid. Even more malevolent is the Affarit jinn. Jul Jenahen is one of these nasty Affarit jinns. He has to be neutralized. The state of affairs in the country is not satisfactory. So many of us Muslims live in Bengal but I hear we shall be ruled by Hindus. The wind carries all the news to me. And now we have this invasion of the jinns. Our community is facing grave danger, my brothers. Infidels on one side, Affarit jinns on the other. All of us must raise our arms towards Allah's court and say, we want peace. Let the infidels not step on our heads, and let the Affarit jinns be destroyed by the power of the Prophet Solaiman.'

'Subhanallah!' agreed the audience.

One of the disciples said, 'A peasant in our village was nabbed by a jinn last week. My sacred lord, he went out to the field at night to till the land. It's a moonlit night. A short man appears on the raised land between the fields, a smile playing on his lips. He may be short, but he's strong, like our Zulfiqar Mian here. The man asks the peasant "Is it tough to till the land these days?" The peasant gets very angry and says, "I'm busting my arse here – is this the time for jokes? Get out of here; go do your own stuff." Shorty says, "Ah, poor man, let me help you with your work, at least it will lessen your burden a bit." Our peasant was very happy. After all, one doesn't get people to work for free. As he ploughs, the peasant notices that Shorty, who resembles Zulfiqar Mian, has hind legs of a goat instead of human limbs. Seeing this he runs away at once and doesn't stop till he reached his village. Only when he sees a fellow human does he regain his confidence. Panting, he says, "You'd have had a fit if you saw what I saw tonight." The other man asks, "What did you see?" The peasant says, "This man I saw said he would help me with my work and came into the field with me, and then his legs...I don't know how to tell you..." The other man points to his own feet and asks, "Like this?" 'Oh Dado re, this man also had goats' hooves for feet! The peasant fainted on the spot.'

Pir Sahib raised his arms and prayed, 'It is all your wish, everything happens according to your plans. Listen, my brothers, Allahtaala has sent angels for all humans. These angels will protect us from jinns and wild animals. On our part we have to pray at Allah's court to keep him happy. We have to obey the pir, and those on whom the jinns have set their sights, like Zulfiqar Mian's friend here, will have to wear amulcts with wolves' teeth, fur, or bones. Jinns cannot stand the stench of wolves. Another thing, no one must kill snakes that live in your homes. If you are afraid of them, ask them to go away. They will leave on their own after three days. If you have a resident snake, nasty jinns are too frightened to visit you. Snakes can see jinns, and they hiss when they do. Black dogs help the angel of death, but snakes kill jinns. If you are terrified, send for an exorcist, lure the snake into a pitcher, cover its mouth and then let the snake out in the fields. But don't kill it, for that will only embolden the jinns. My advice to German Mian, and to all of you – Hazrat Mohammad, peace be upon him, declared that the human race will have to perform seven kinds of activities and stay away from seven kinds of other activities. What are these?

You have to look after sick people, you have to serve your mother, you have to participate in the ritual preparations for burials, and you have to cover the grave with earth too. If you see anyone straying from the true path, you have to bring them back. You have to greet your Muslim brothers. And you have to honour invitations from anyone who asks you for a meal – you cannot demean them because they are poor. Allah will be angry.

What must you not do?

Do not wear anything made of gold. Do not drink water from a silver bowl. Do not touch silk. Do not wear expensive clothes. Do not put on a silk pirhan. Do not dress in a kurta with embroidery. And do not touch brocade.

'Repeat after me, Alhamdulillah!'

Alhamdulillah, echoed everyone in praise of the lord.

German Mian whispered in Zulfiqar Ali's ear, 'Is Jinnah a jinn, then?'

Zulfiqar Ali laughed. 'He's not a jinn, he's human.'

Pir Sahib did not hold court very long on Thursdays. He would leave soon, after which the audience could go home. Since he remained seated, the disciples began to converse among themselves. German Mian wondered whether the jinns had indeed set their sights on him, or whether these were bad dreams born of ill fortune. Did this Pir Sahib or Zulfiqar Ali know how to interpret dreams? He needed to know the meaning of his dreams. But he wasn't thinking of getting rid of them. What would he live on if that happened?

Once Pir Sahib left, his disciples began to disperse. German Mian and Zulfiqar Mian were in a hurry too. They would have to bathe and then visit the mosque. It was Friday. If the mosque got too crowded they would be forced to read the namaz on the road. To find room inside, they would have to reach early. There were no distinctions here between the rich and the poor. German Mian fired a light barb at Zulfiqar Ali. 'Do you read the Jumma namaz at home too?' The Jumma namaz could not be read by oneself at home, it was just not possible. Realizing that this was not a joke but a dart intended for him, Zulfiqar Ali at once launched a counter-attack. 'Let's not speak about it, the sermons they read in your mosques here in Hindustan are not even worth listening to. I hear these Khutbas invoking some ancient Caliph or Sultan. Is this our religion? Go to Turkey, the sermon invokes Caliph Abdul Maqid.' German Mian said, 'But he's been dead two years. And Kemal Ataturk expelled this Caliph twenty or twenty-five years ago. It's best to love the country you live in, Mian. Don't bring up the Turkish connection all the time.'

Annoyed, Zulfiqar Mian said, 'You Sunnis will never accept defeat. You could invoke the twelfth Imam instead. We Alevis favour this move.'

German Mian smiled. He had not expected Zulfikar Ali to fall into his trap so quickly. He felt compelled to strike back. 'But you Shias don't even acknowledge the first three Caliphs – you only acknowledge the twelve Imams. You even refer to the fourth Caliph as the first Imam. You people are Shia Alevis, who enjoy music and dance, who do not like going to the mosque – but one of them is now to be found regularly at the shrine of Shah Rustam, who was a descendant of the first Caliph, Hazrat Abu Bakr. Am I wrong?'

Zulfiqar Ali appeared to have been prepared with his answer. 'If you people can go through the Matam ritual of lamentation and breast-beating at Muharram despite being Sunnis, if you can accept the Ahl-al-Bayt – the five holy personalities of Nabiji, Hazrat Ali, Ma Fatima, Hasan and Husain –what's wrong with our going to the shrine? The heart of the matter Mian, is that we are all the same. The British are trying to instigate us into fighting and killing one another. Let me tell you, I know someone who can interpret your dreams. There isn't anyone here who doesn't know Bade. His real name is Mullah Badreddoza. The blessings of Hazrat Yusuf, peace be upon him, are with him.'

German Mian was over the moon with joy. There was a great deal more he would have said; the argument would not have ended so quickly. But now, forgetting the conflict, he requested Zulfiqar Mian, 'Can you invite him home this evening?'

'Yes, that's what I thought I'd do. He lives in the village of Kuluri, which is next to ours. A mile or so away – about fifteen minutes on foot. I will send someone to fetch him after the namaz. If no one's available I'll go myself.'

Zulfiqar Ali disappeared at the end of Jumma. He wasn't to be seen at the Asr namaz in the afternoon either. Perhaps he was off to fetch Badreddoza, or had gone off on some business of his own. German Mian spent a lonely day. He leafed through some of the books in the front room, but did not feel inclined to read any of them. Once or twice he tried to eavesdrop on conversations between the women in Zulfiqar Mian's inner chambers, but he controlled himself the very next moment. Zulfiqar Mian's childless wife might be pouring out her woes to a maid, it would be wrong, he felt, to overhear her.

Evening rode in on the Magrib azaan, and with it Zulfiqar Mian appeared too, accompanied by Mullah Badreddoza.

It was decided that Bade Mullah would spend the night here. He would sleep along with German Mian in the front room. The plump man was both courageous and pious. He kept people enthralled with his stories. This, roughly, is what Mullah Badreddoza said before going to bed that night:

'When a jeweller makes ornaments, he engraves different patterns on them. When selling the ornaments, he recovers a steep price from the customer for those patterns. And why not, considering the effort he has put into it? If the buyer comes back to him to sell it during a crisis, the jeweller pays only for the gold, without offering a paise for the patterns. Things that are valuable when they are sold have no value when they are bought – except gold. This is how to tell the real apart from the fake. German Mian, too will have to distinguish between the real and the false in his dreams. For instance, the dream about Robin. The person who had appeared to be Robin in the darkness was not actually Robin, but someone with inverted elbows and knees. It wasn't clear whether it was a human or a jinn. Even though he appeared to be advancing, he was actually retreating and vice versa. Where was he going, or where was he coming from? Islam pays a lot of attention to this business of coming and going. It talks of the past and the future. Wherever you look, all you see is the past and the future. There is no such thing as the present. German Mian's dream at half-light was the same. The present is actually an illusion, which the British refer to as magic and the Hindus as indrajal – a web spun by the king of the gods. Its objective is not to trap insects, but to trap humans. The sacred Quran Sharif says this magic is forbidden and since we're talking of magic, we cannot but tell the story of Haroot and Maroot. Only then will the meaning of Mian Sahib's dreams be revealed. It's all a game of patterns. And while on the subject of patterns or naqsha, let me tell you that I am a Naqshbandi dervish. I live in extreme poverty, whether you believe it or not. You may think I'm referring to poverty to gain some mileage or sympathy. We do not belong to that tradition. Unlike Mullahs, we do not covet riches. We are happy being poor, our system is known as the Chisti gharana. You must have heard of the town of Herat in Afghanistan, which was bombed by the British, killing many people. There is a small town next to Herat, which no one knows about. Its name is Chist. That's where our system was founded. A great man named Abu Ishaq Shami was the founding father of the gharana. All of you know of Khwaja Garib Nawaz – he belonged to our gharana too.

'We were talking of patterns, weren't we? But I cannot do justice to the subject unless I mention the ziqr, the practice of reciting the names of god. There's just one thing I have to say. We recite the names of the lord quietly, not loudly. The guru of our guru was Hazrat Abu Bakr. And his guru was Nabiji, the favourite of the world that follows the deen, the righteous way. Oh, but I forgot to tell you about Haroot and Maroot. More on the patterns later. Let me first tell you the story of Haroot and Maroot.

'While the tribes of Israil were enslaved in Babylon, Allahtaala sent a pair of angels to test their faith. Just like the beautiful young boys whose form the angels took to visit the tribe of Hazrat Ibrahim's brother-in-law, let peace be upon him, so too did the lord's angels take the form of a pir and a fakir when they appeared before the Israilis. They set up shop in the marketplace of conjurors and magicians and displayed their skills, warning people, "We are here to test you, the lord has sent us. Don't throw away your afterlife under the influence of magic." But the people paid no attention. They began to practise sifli amliyat, black magic consisting of base tricks and illusions, the use of amulets and spells. Like mad men they began to believe in magic, which the devil had passed off as Prophet Sulaiman's doing. King Sulaiman had never walked the path of heathenism – the devils had done that. They were the ones who taught magic to humans. Some sort of revelation targeting the two angels, Haroot and Maroot, was made, which attracted them to magic. And yet it was the angels who had warned everyone against this. Humans learnt from angels how to create a chasm between husband and wife. They sold their afterlives in exchange for magic.

'The devil had wanted to blame the prophet Sulaiman for the art of magic. As humans respected this prophet and loved him dearly, passing it off as his art would make it easily acceptable and make humans stray from the path of goodness. Hazrat Daud's son Sulaiman had said, "We have been taught the language of birds, oh humans! Allahtaala has granted us all kinds of talents. These are his gifts." Khudataala had formed armies of jinns, humans and birds for the prophet. As he advanced with his soldiers, the ants were frightened. A small ant said, "Let us hide in our holes, or else the prophet Sulaiman's soldiers will trample all over us. We will die." The prophet Sulaiman understood them. He could decipher the speech of all beasts and birds in the universe. He used to love the entire animal kingdom and take care of them. Once, he became very worried when the hoopoe bird went missing, and said, "He will have to explain where he has vanished." The bird had in fact flown off to bring back news from another world – the world of a queen named Sabah. Sabah's other name was Bilqis. No one in her kingdom prostrated themselves for the sacred lords, they considered the sun as their God.

The hoopoe brought this information back to the prophet Sulaiman, who became suspicious and sent a messenger to Bilqis's kingdom. The queen had heard of king Sulaiman, and sent back expensive gifts with great reverence, saying, "All these are my offerings to the king." The prophet did not accept them, telling the messenger, "Return these. Allah has given me gifts far more precious." Neither the powerful jinns nor learned men could appease him with gifts. Now the queen's messenger came to Sulaiman. "What is this gift that is more valuable than Queen Bilkis's, oh king?" he asked. Ilam – Learning, answered the prophet. The sacred lord himself had taught the prophet Sulaiman. This was the finest gift in the world.

'Christians say that Queen Bilqis visited Sulaiman herself. They even talked to each other. Listen to their conversation:

'Queen Bilqis asked, "What is it that is bad, oh King?"

'Prophet Sulaiman answered, "The great lord's eyes are everywhere. He determines what is good and what is bad as required and tells his servant as much. To hear it, you need a heart, a heart that is devoted to Khudataala."

'Queen: Which is more powerful, the eyes or the ears?

'Prophet: The eyes are for seeing and the ears, for hearing. He created both. The servant decides how deaf or blind he wants to be.

'Queen: Which part of the body is the most powerful?

'Prophet: The tongue.

'Queen: How do the body and the soul co-exist, oh King?

'Prophet: The body is the home of the soul, and the soul is the real form of the body.

'Queen: Of ten doors, if one is open the other nine are closed. And if the other nine are open, one is closed. What is this?

'Prophet: The pregnant woman's womb. The ten doors are a pair of eyes, two ears, two nostrils, the mouth, the anus, the penis or vagina, and the navel. In the mother's womb only the child's navel is open, all the others are closed. When the child emerges, the navel closes and the other nine open.

'Queen: Seven leave, nine arrive. Two provide warmth, one feeds.

'Prophet: Seven days – the menstrual period. Nine months – pregnancy. A pair of breasts for warmth and one for feeding.'

Mullah Badreddoza's temperament was like Zulfiqar Mian's. He didn't know when to stop. Not that his stories weren't a pleasure to listen to. Next he started narrating the story of the prophet Sulaiman's dreams.

'The prophet's father passed away when he was very young. One night prophet Sulaiman dreamt that the lord was telling him "What do you wish for, Sulaiman, tell me." The prophet Sulaiman answered "My father was devoted to the principles of religion and very special to your heart. There was no stain on his character. He was a learned and honest man. That is why your compassion was showered on him like a revelation. Now I am the king instead of him at this green age. I am so young that

I do not know what I should do and what I should stay away from. I am king to countless living beings. Not just humans but other animals also live in my realm. I do not know if I have the knowledge to ensure the good of everyone in this vast kingdom. I might harm one creature in the course of helping another. Grant me the ability to tell the difference between good and bad, between well-being and harm, for everyone. There is nothing else I wish for. "Exceedingly pleased with this request, Khudataala said, "You have not asked for a long lifetime for yourself, you have not asked for the annihilation of your enemies, you have only asked for an understanding of justice. I am granting you this knowledge. I will fill your mind with Al-adalah, the sense of justice. You shall be the finest among the learned; knowledge will be your asset. Along with these I grant you earthly riches and honour. No emperor shall be your equal in your lifetime. If you stay on my path, as your father did, I shall grant you a long life too.'"

Badreddoza said, 'Solaiman Mian's dream was a divine revelation.' Touching his forehead with his fingertips he continued, 'The divine revelation was made to Hazrat Mohammad, peace be upon him, through a dream too. This sort of dream is one part out of the forty-six of prophethood. Let me tell you why. The first revelation was made over six months, and it lasted twenty-three years. Two six-month periods add up to one year. So twenty-three years amount to forty-six periods of six months each, and that is why dreams are referred to as one part out of forty-six of prophethood. But not any old dream. This sort of dream is called the Rahmani dream.

There are three kinds of dreams in the world – Rahmani, Nafsani and Shaitani. The Rahmani dream comes from the lord. Nafsani dreams are created within human minds. And the Shaitani kind come from Iblis and his associates.'

He continued, 'German Mian's dreams belong to the Nafsani kind. The sacred soul that resides within the body is sometimes split into two – it even breaks into many pieces at times. That is when dreams descend in droves. These are not revelations. Truths about one's land, stories of pain in the family, and all kinds of unfulfilled wishes manifest themselves as Nafsani dreams, prowling the night. Just as a man's life does not run according to his own wishes, similarly he cannot kill or suppress dreams. Apparently we have been given the freedom to do as we please in this life. Granted, but how extensive is this freedom? After death even this little bit of freedom is taken away. Now move backwards. Before being born a human being has a life too – in his mother's womb. When Allah grants him a soul, this innocent child arrives in the world after writhing in the warm water of the womb. Then begins his human life, lasting till death. Between death and judgment day he goes to barzakh, where good people lie in a cold sleep while evil people are tormented. On judgment day, good deeds and sins are weighed against one another. In the Maidan-e-Hashr, the field of resurrection, there are no brothers or friends, wives and children are all non-entities.

Behesht and Dozakh, heaven and hell, are unending places of unending time where humans have no free will. So where then do their wishes reside? All within those Nafsani dreams.

'Never mind all that. The more I talk, the more likely I am to forget what is important. I have identified a house for German Mian in our village in Haaripara. It's cheap and secluded. Once the Hindus leave from Harinya village next door, everything will become dirt cheap. You can then buy something else according to your preference. The Hindus will have to leave if Pakistan is formed. This is what I just can't accept. Think about it my friends, the man whom I see every morning when I go for a shit, whom I smile at as I move a little further away to urinate, will no longer be there. Is this supposed to make me happy? Hari Pandit is a friend of my father's. I still consider him a father figure. Are he and I supposed to become enemies and live in separate countries? Zulfiqar Mian might be a foreigner, but German Mian belongs to this country, a different district. Why don't you speak up, what is it that you want? Maybe they won't pay any attention to peasants like us but you are an aristocrat. All of you should tell them loudly what you, what we, want. Pardon my insolence. I have a quick temper. You are more learned than I am. Never mind all this. Bhabi Saheba and beti will be here in a day or two. I have sent word to Mejo Mian as Zulfiqar Mian asked me to. We won't let you go.'

German Mian felt a little apprehensive at all this. It was true that he did not want to return to the place where he had seen the corpse, but how was he to run his household in these unfamiliar surroundings? He had not had to do it all these years. He could sell his share of land back home and buy something here, but what would happen to his cherished horses? Would he be able to bring them over? The snail, in whose form he had been climbing all over the corpse last night without finding what he was looking for, appeared again in his mind's eye. Suddenly he heard hoof beats. But he was awake!

Badreddoza surmised from German Mian's expression that something was wrong. Nudging him, he asked, 'What are you thinking about?'

'Horses,' came German Mian's reply.

'Then let me talk of a different kind of pattern. I'll give you a puzzle to solve...This one is regarding horses. A boy named Farid was told by his father as he was about to die "Farid, here are my seventeen horses, and there are three of you brothers. You're the eldest, the only one who earns. So you must do the division. You will take half the horses, give two-thirds of the rest to your younger brother, and one-ninth of the total number to your little brother."

'You will go mad trying to work it out. How can you get a half of seventeen? And that too when it's to do with horses. If they had been cows they could have been slaughtered and the meat divided up. The other divisions are difficult too. But Farid knew the ways of the Naqshbandis. He fulfilled his father's wish easily by playing the numbers.

'Farid had a horse of his own. He added it to the pool. There will be no miscalculation here, you can check for yourself. He took nine out of the eighteen. Of the nine left, two-thirds – six horses – went to his younger brother and two – one-ninth of eighteen – went to the little brother. That left one horse, which was his own to begin with, and he rode it back home. You could say this isn't correct mathematics but I will say, if you look carefully, no one lost, and everyone gained.'

~ *Dar-us-Salam* ~

ABODE OF PEACE

Barely had German Mian settled down in his new house than a new menace began to infest the village. It wasn't rioting or violence, but was still a matter of concern. Especially to a new resident like German Mian, who normally had a calm temperament, and was a coward to boot. His unease was multiplied a thousand fold.

Two strangers began to appear frequently in the village. They barged into people's homes, even into their bedrooms at times. Their clothing and behaviour were most mysterious.

After moving into this house German Mian had been possessed by a couple of new addictions, although all that was forgotten now.

The first of the addictions was the gramophone. A few days ago his brother had sent him a record of a song sung by Kundanlal Saigal and Aamir Bai. The morning always began with this song:

'Kya hamne bigara hai
Kyun hamein satate ho…

Hum khelenge jis dil se

Us dil ko chhupate ho...'

'What have I done to you for you to torment me? Why do you hide the heart I want to play with...'

The second addiction was a woman behind purdah. Opening the window on the southern side of German Mian's bedroom brought in a gust of cold wind over the pond. But looking beyond the pond made his body and heart tingle. What did that woman do all day on the opposite bank of the pond? Why did she spend most of the day on the steps leading down to the water? German Mian saw her do the dishes sometimes, or wash clothes. But that didn't take very much time. She pretended to work much more than she actually did. This too was a mystery he could not unravel. But German Mian did not like her absence either. A pregnant Kamrunnesa spent most of her time resting in the next room. The baby would be born any day now. The local midwife had already visited several times. Someone in such an advanced state of pregnancy was not supposed to do any housework. His brother had sent a couple of people to do the domestic chores. Even in this village, there was no lack of people who would work without pay for two square meals a day.

German Mian's days had been passing pleasantly, but this menace of the two strangers had him worried. Whenever anyone asked them a question, they vanished like a magic act. It wasn't as though there were no strangers to be found in the village. Hawkers and beggars were obviously unfamiliar people. But these two did not belong to that category. They were dressed in glittering robes with embroidered gold and silver threads, wore Sulaimani rings and carried the flags of Pir Ilyas. No one could fathom why they were visiting the village. Was something terrible about to happen hereabout?

German Mian usually wasn't one to fret over such things – there were worthier men than him to do the worrying. Along with his dreams, he was enraptured by the music and by the woman in purdah by the pond. But this single-mindedness was disrupted by the two mysterious men. One day German Mian actually ran into the two youngsters. 'Assalamo alaikum,' he said apprehensively. Instead of replying, they said angrily 'Was it right to abandon the corpse? No burial, no rituals on the fourth and the fortieth days!' A trembling German Mian was about to apologise when they disappeared in a flash.

He did not dare open the south-facing window that day. He didn't feel like playing Saigal-Aamir Bai either. Instead, the gramophone played:

'Dil jalta hai to jalne de
Aansu na baha fariyaad na kar
Tu parda nasheen ka aashiq hai
Yoon naam-e-vafa barbaad na kar
Dil jalta hai to jalne de
Maasoom nazar ke teer chala
Bismil ko Bismil aur bana
Ab sharm-o-haya ke parde mein
Tuchhup chhup ke...'

'Let the heart suffer if it must, don't staunch the tears. Don't dishonor your love who's behind the veil, let your wounds grow deeper, let the heart suffer if it must…'

Mukesh's tear-laced voice wrenched his heart. He grew pensive, wistful. Already in this state of mind, thoughts of the two strangers and the results of the Bengal elections further blurred his view of his dreams for a few days. Having created this hazy vision of a Milky Way obscured by clouds, German Mian plunged into deep thought.

Having won more seats than the Krishak Praja Party and the Congress, the Muslim League would form the government. This was a matter of great joy. The League had won 113 out of the 250 seats in the state, the Congress had won 86 and the others 47. The League needed 13 more seats to gain a simple majority. The Hindu Mahasabha had won a few seats but it would not support the League. And even if it did, it would be idiotic for the League to form a government with its support. The League did not want to ally with the Krishak Praja Party either. That left the Congress. It was likely a coalition government would be formed, killing two birds with one stone. First the enemy, the Hindu Mahasabha and the Krishak Praja Party, would be cornered so they wouldn't be able to assert themselves. And second, an alliance between the Muslim League and the Congress would avert the possibility of riots. But German Mian knew that it wasn't as though the Hindu Mahasabha and the Krishak Praja Party were not in covert touch with the Congress at the grassroots level. Take

Murshidabad – the Congress had won three seats, the Muslim League two, and an Independent had won the sixth seat. This independent candidate, Khuda Bux, was actually a Congress supporter. Ostensibly the Congress had left this seat to the Hindu Mahasabha, but secretly they had nominated Khuda Bux, who was masquerading as an independent candidate.

What also worried German Mian was the fact that the Hindu Mahasabha's candidates were in second place in terms of votes polled in three of the six constituencies. This growth of the Mahasabha in a Muslim-majority area did not appear particularly propitious. It meant that Hindus had teamed up to boost the Mahasabha's votes, while the Muslim vote had been split between the League, the Krishak Praja Party and the Congress. Had the League won all these votes the picture would have changed, but no matter how much Muslims talked of unity it was evident that this was not reflected in their actions. This was how Muslims were losing out the world over; who could save a community that did not want to save itself? But just the fact that it did not seem propitious would not change anything. Fazlul Haq's support for Shyamaprasad Mukherjee had spelt ruin not just for himself but also for Bengal's Muslims.

Fazlul Haq was perfectly familiar with the technicalities of the law. He was only the second Muslim from the subcontinent to have earned a law degree. But he couldn't stand up to Shyamaprasad Mukherjee when it came to the shrewd machinations of politics. The community hung its head in shame when reminded of the way in which Mukherjee-babu had made an ass of Haq Sahib in the coalition. German Mian felt his blood boil with rage whenever he considered how Haq Sahib, who was at heart a Congressman, had ensured the decline of Bengal's Muslims. But what use was rage? Now that the Hindu Mahasabha had been allowed to have the upper hand, weakening it would be quite arduous. Besides, the Mahasabha was quite influential beyond Bengal too. They received funds from various places. Just like vultures flocking around a carcass, the lure of money always brought people rushing in. If the country were to be partitioned in these circumstances, there would be considerable doubt whether Murshidabad would be allotted to Pakistan or not. But there was no doubt about the fact that Bengal was about to get a Muslim League government. It was also certain that the government would not include either the Krishak Praja Party or the Mahasabha. The two League candidates who had won in Murshidabad, Murtaza Reza Chowdhury and Prince Kasem Ali Mirza, were both believed to be competent people. The entire district had reposed its hope and trust in them.

German Mian surmised that the two strangers wandering around the village were probably Prince Kasem Ali and Murtaza Reza. But why would they behave this way in their own area? Was German Mian going mad? Confronted by this suspicion, he turned to Kamrunnesa Bibi, who could solve all problems. She was busy reading the novel *Jahanara.* Saudamini, also known as Jahanara, was seated by the Pir Sahib's lake. On the other side of the lake stood a Satyanarayan temple. Hindus and Muslims lived side by side happily in the village of Meherpur. German Mian sat down next to Kamrunnesa. Putting her book aside, Kamrunnesa asked, 'What news, Chhoto Mian?'

She laughed uproariously when German Mian asked whether the mysterious pair lurking in the village were Prince Kasem Ali and Murtaza Reza. Kamrennusa had probably forgotten for a few moments that women were not supposed to laugh loudly. Reminded of this when she saw German Mian's expression, she turned serious again, asking, 'Are you under the impression they are hovering around here to help the cause of your cherished Pakistan? Do you suppose Allahtaala's wrath has descended on them? Are you dreaming again, Mian? I'll have to send word to Mejo Bhaijan.'

German Mian lapsed into silence. What did she mean, send word to his brother. She said whatever she liked. Where had his wife learnt to talk so freely? She had no home of her own to speak of. It was his brother's indulgence that had made Kamrennusa such a formidable figure today. Besides, words weren't taxed which was why people remained unscathed no matter what they said. At any other time he would have shouted loudly enough to be heard in every house in the neighbourhood but he did not dare scream at someone who was eight or nine months pregnant. Not just Kamrunnesa but also the child in her womb would also be subjected to his screams and his burden of sins would grow heavier. A helpless German Mian went back to his own room and switched on the gramophone.

'Kya hamne bigara hai
Kyun humko satate ho…
Hum khelenge jis dil se
Us dil ko chhupate ho...'

Even if German Mian did not know Murtaza Reza, who belonged to the famous zamindar family of Kotalpur in Jangipur, he knew Kasem Ali quite well. Ali was the son of a nawab, and calling him the 'jewel of the Muslim League' in this district would be an understatement. Everyone hereabout referred to him as 'Ratan' Ali Mirza, Prince 'Ratan' Ali. His father Wasef Ali Mirza was still fighting desperately to save his status as a nawab. He owed the British sixteen lakh rupees. It was doubtful whether he could return it even by selling his estate. And if he were to lose power he would be turned into a beggar. He was continuing his opposition to the Partition so that his debt could be written off and his coffers remain untouched. His son Kasem Ali couldn't be bothered with any of this. Being a courageous young man, he had enrolled with the League and was now on the rampage. Nawab Wasef Ali owned a great deal of property in the Rajsahi district of east Bengal. His holdings in Srihatta and Khulna were not small either. The nawab would suffer terrible losses if the country were to be partitioned and Murshidabad was allotted to India, which was why he was now busy organizing meetings with Hindus and Muslims alike. Critics said that the father had deliberately pushed the son into the League, asking him to ensure that Murshidabad was allotted to Pakistan. If there was no partition, his estate would be saved. Even if the country was partitioned, and Murshidabad, Rajsahi and Srihatta all went to Pakistan, his estate would still remain in one piece. He wouldn't have to give up anything except his place in the government of Hindustan. This was the best he could hope for, for if there was a partition and Murshidabad were to be in Hindustan, that would be the end of his status as a nawab. That was why he was busy holding meetings jointly with Hindus and Muslims, and why he was thought to have nudged his third son to join the League and ensure that Murshidabad stayed with Pakistan. Kasem Ali Mirza was not particularly worried about nawabhood, for he had two elder brothers. The eldest of them would inherit the estate. Only by joining the League could he hope to have the dice of power rolling his way. The nawab's elder sons Wares Ali Mirza and Fateh Yaar Ali Mirza steered completely clear of politics. They were steeped in a life of pleasure. But their brows were creased with worry now. Of the dozen children of the nawab only Kasem Sahib had stepped up to do something for the betterment of the community, whatever the critics may say. The public at large was terming it a father-versus-son feud. They wanted to find out who the victor would be. Whom would Murshidabad go to? Hindustan, asserted the father while the son wanted it to be part of Pakistan. The son wasn't always able to match up to his father. Nawab Wasef Ali was a tiger. He had degrees from Rugby and from Trinity College at Oxford. His son was an intellectual pygmy in comparison. He had an array of titles –

Mohabbat-e-Jung, Aamir-ul-Umrah, Rais-ud-Daulah, Ihtisham-ul-Mulk, Night Commander. A man like this might not be able to stop the country from being partitioned, but he would not allow Murshidabad to become part of Pakistan. He had even said at meetings and parades that the people of Pakistan would not understand the worth of the Hazarduari palace. Nawab Bahadur was a Shia Muslim, which meant that he should have joined the Muslim League. But if rumours were to be believed, Wasef Ali Mirza was a patriot. What other rationale could there be behind his decision to support the Congress? Let the critics say what they liked, many people agreed that the nawab was a true lover of his country. It seems he had accepted Maulana Abul Kalam Azad as his guru. However, Kasem Ali Mirza a Shia, and Murtaza Sahib a Sunni, had pledged their hearts that they would get Murshidabad to be part of Pakistan.

It was a different picture in Bengal though. The Congress and the League, sworn enemies, were apparently trying to form a coalition government. Congress leader Kiran Shankar Roy was holding secret meetings with the League. It was being hotly rumored that the Congress would support the League. But every Tom, Dick and Harry couldn't expect an audience with Kiran Shankar Roy. He was an important man, a heavyweight. A professor by profession, he taught at Presidency College. A descendant of the Taonta royal family of Manikganj, he had taken charge of the Congress in Bengal after completing his education at Oxford. Since his party was in second place with 86 seats it had some claims of its own in order to be part of a coalition government. For instance, the party wanted half the ministerial posts. The problem was that all 113 Muslim League winners were expecting to be ministers. So a meeting was convened between the Muslim League and the Congress to end the impasse. But who among the senior leaders of the League enjoyed the trust of the Congress? Suhrawardy did not want to join the negotiations. He dispatched his wife for the talks. A Russian woman would decide how many ministerial posts could be given to the Congress!

Suhrawardy's first wife Niaz Fatima had died nearly twenty-five years ago. He had then married a Russian dancer. Although she lived in Russia, his wife's ancestors came from Poland. She had learnt acting from Olga Knipper at the Moscow Art Theatre. People knew Olga less as an actor-director and more as Anton Chekov's wife. Suhrwarady's new wife had married Eugene Tiscenko while acting in the Moscow Art Theatre. Eugene belonged to the Greek Orthodox Church. Tiscenko and Suhrawardy's current wife had a son too, whose name was Oleg; Chekov's former wife Olga had chosen the name. Eugene Tiscenko and Vera Alexandrovonvona Tiscenko Calder's marriage was far from happy. She ran away to Calcutta with the Director of the Moscow Art Theatre, Sir Hasan Shahid Suhrawardy. But instead of the man she had come with, she went on to fall in love with Hussain Shahid Suhrawardy, and began to live with the uncle.

The colourful, intelligent and witty Hussain Suhrawardy did not escape Vera's attention, an Oxford graduate, a renowned barrister and to top it all, a member of the legislative assembly. In Calcutta, Vera had been paying for herself and her son out of her own income. Suhrawardy's brother and uncle had provided support, but she was an independent minded woman. Ignoring the man whose help she had sought to escape from Russia, she also ignored his widower uncle and reached out to the jewel in the crown, taking a number of important steps to cement the relationship.

Once she was in Calcutta, Vera converted to Islam following her proximity to the Suhrawardy family. Her son Oleg also grew up in accordance with his mother's faith. Vera wrote to her husband Eugene to inform him of the nobility of Islam and invited him to convert too, but the fanatical young Christian refused and requested that his son be brought up under the Greek Orthodox faith. Now Vera made a different move by going to the court in Calcutta. Since the Suhrawardy family was well-versed in the law, Vera Alexandrovonvona Tiscenko Calder wasted no time in seeking their help in the matter.

All the newspapers in Calcutta and rest of India covered this one exciting news. Its legal, social, political and international reach was extensive. The Indian newspapers wrote:

'A Polish woman who is a citizen of Russia married a young Russian man who is a Greek Orthodox Christian. The wedding was held in Germany. The same woman has now converted to Islam and is trying to annul her marriage in a Calcutta court.'

The marriage eventually fell apart. And the man credited

with this accomplishment was Hussain Shahid Suhrawardy. Vera, also known as Begum Noorjahan, was head over heels in love. This new name had been given to her by the Imam of the Nakhoda mosque after he had converted her. Suhrawardy had noticed however that Noorjahan was not as attached to Islam as she was attracted to the Bahai faith. She had professed her love for him only because she wanted to remain in proximity to power, marrying him too for the same reason. But he couldn't afford to be distracted by such trivialities. He wanted to reach the pinnacle of power. He simply had to become the prime minister of Bengal. The partitioning of India would be excellent news for him. He wanted to make use of Noorjahan. Many of India's politicians would be charmed by a white woman, especially one who had taken the responsibility for bargaining on behalf of the Muslim League.

Regular meetings were being held between Begum Noorjahan and the Congress leader Kiranshankar Roy, who belonged to the royal family of Manikganj. Noorjahan didn't capitulate when Kiran-babu proved inflexible, and secretly secured the support of the European Union. And Lieutenant Governor General Sir Frederick John Burrows invited Hussain Shahid Suhrawardy to form the government.

Would it really have been terrible for the Congress and the Muslim League to have arrived at an agreement, wondered German Mian. Somewhere a ray of hope had been getting brighter. A few more meetings could have done no harm. If the Praja Party and the Mahasabha could have an alliance, why couldn't the Congress and the League have one too? It would have quelled the excesses of the Hindu Mahasabha. But it was wrong to expect all this. How was Pakistan to be formed if this were to materialize? Therefore, what Allahtaala did was always for the best. The League had not taken much time to form the government. They would wait and watch to find out whether Bengal would see a revival. Squeezed between the famine and politics, things were in a sorry state.

Meanwhile, German Mian no longer saw the woman in purdah by the pond, working or pretending to work when he opened the window to the south. He didn't listen to Aamir Bai and Saigal's song very often these days. His dreams had turned bitter and peculiar over the past few days. He was forced to tell Mullah Badreddoza that his visits to Shah Rustam's shrine were responsible for this. He had lost his real, pure dreams over there. He no longer had exchanges with Jul Jenahen or nymphs. He wondered who or what had infected his blood with thoughts of national politics and everyday survival. He wasn't pleased with this situation at all, although his brother Anwar Mian was bound to be happy with this transformation, concluding that he had brought his younger brother to the right place. But he would be very upset that the Congress and the League had not formed an alliance in Bengal. Anwar Mian was a staunch supporter of the Congress. He had always said that an alliance would prevent partition. Would it have mattered very much had Kiran-babu accepted the conditions set by the League? But German Mian did not know what these conditions were. People were even saying that Kiran-babu and his party were ready to join the government, but the problem was with Begum Noorjahan. Had someone else attended the meetings with the Congress instead of her, the League-Congress alliance would certainly have materialized. Begum Noorjahan had apparently kept asserting herself strongly throughout the meetings. She considered Bengal similar to the Moscow Art Theatre. There she had had Olga Knipper and here her mentor was Hussain Shahid Suhrawardy himself. The members of the League were saying that Kiranshankar Roy was already dismayed with the disputes over his family's land in Manikganj. His anxiety had taken its toll on these meetings. A young man named Bijon Bhattacharya had become an overnight sensation in Calcutta with his play on the famine, and this young playright's kinsfolk were battling it out with the kings of Manikganj for rights over land there. Babar Ali, a skilled stick-fighter had annexed Kiranshankar's ancestors' land on some islands that had surfaced on the Padma. This Babar Ali was the principal member of the private army of Bijon Bhattacharya's grandfather, Rashbehari Bhattacharya.

Although German Mian's dreams had turned bitter and peculiar, they were just as troublesome as before, and stark reality could not dispel his discomfort. In this situation German Mian decided that henceforth he would visit Shah Makhdum Abdul Hamid's shrine instead of Shah Rustam's. Accordingly, he sent for Badreddoza. He had been hearing of the potency of this particular shrine. Praying there brought results for both

Muslims and Hindus. Seventy-five per cent of the visitors at Shah Makhdum Abdul Hamid's shrine were Hindu, and the rest were Muslim. It was situated very close to the Salar railway station, which wasn't far from German Mian's house – it was a fifteen-minute walk. But even such a wonderful shrine did not bring peace to German Mian. In fact, he felt quite frightened at these potent shrines. Something like the fear of ghosts during childhood. It was in this eerie setting that a Khadim, with a pair of tongs in his hand and drooping eyes, dressed in a multicolored patchwork robe, got hold of him. German Mian looked around wildly for Badreddoza, but he was nowhere to be seen. They had arrived here together... Where had he disappeared, leaving German Mian to fend for himself? Suddenly the Khadim yelled, 'Shut up you insolent fellow!' The next moment he lowered his voice and squeaked like a mouse, 'Give me some money, I haven't eaten for days, I'll pray for whatever you want.'

A little nervous, German Mian took a coin out of his pocket and handed it over, hoping to secure his release. He whispered in the Khadim's ear, 'Pray for the formation of Pakistan my father.' The tong-wielding Khadim said, 'What Pakistan, whose Pakistan? I can pray for Hindustan my son, I don't support fighting. Take your money back.'

Trying to get away quickly, German Mian tripped on a stone and the big toe of his right foot began to bleed profusely. Looking closely, German Mian discovered that the nail had almost come off. There was no house nearby that he could turn to for first-aid. It was hurting terribly too. What else could the Tong Khadim do to him! To German Mian, he appeared quite mad, but not harmful. The incident frightened Tong Khadim so much, however, that he ran away. German Mian called out Badreddoza's name loudly, but he was nowhere to be seen. Someone sang from inside the shrine the lyrics talking of strange, secret things lurking hot and irresistibly in the blood. It ended:

'Listen to my advice, my boy,

You're just a child in this colourful world...'

German Mian was astonished. He had never imagined he would hear such sophisticated music in this locality. What incredible poetry! Who was it who was singing? Whose voice was the source of such polished observations? They sounded like lines from a folk song of the wise. He had certainly not expected to hear a song like this, but was there anything that the sacred lord's infinite compassion could not achieve? The Tong Khadim reappeared suddenly, holding a filthy red rag. Tearing off a scrap, he set fire to it, and using the ash to bandage German Mian's wound he said, 'Ganja ash. You'll be fine in a couple of days. But this Hamidhaati area will not go to Pakistan.' German Mian's head was bursting with pain. Tong Khadim slipped away suddenly, returning with several things in his hand. He pulled out some ganja, prepared a chilam and lit up. After several drags he held it out to German Mian, saying, 'Have a smoke. Everything will be fine.'

The two of them sat beneath an ancient banyan for a smoke.

Its aerial roots descended to the ground all around them. At any other time German Mian would have swung to and fro on them but he could not do that now. He was quite sick. Besides, the area around the shrine did not appear normal. A hissing sound was floating in from somewhere, was it the wind or a snake? The area seemed clearer because of the smoke from the ganja. Another song wafted in gently, though it wasn't obvious whether it was from the heart of the shrine or from the world on the other side of the tree.

German Mian felt that someone had looked into his heart – be it Makhdoom Sahib or the world beyond the banyan tree. For what could explain such music otherwise? What was he seeking – was it just a male child? Kamrunnesa would have her baby any day now. Would he not have a son this time too? 'Thorns in the flower bed, the heart locked up' – was Makhdoom Shah singing of the woman in purdah on the far side of the pond? No, he would have to keep the south-facing window closed forever and hold Allah's name in his heart instead.

German Mian wept. Whether it was because of the tears or the ganja, German Mian could clearly see that his heart – which the people of this area called 'Bismillah' – was being pulverized after being broken, and this heart of his, white like a shroud, had mingled with the smoke from the ganja to create an ethereal web of illusion here in the yard of the shrine. Through the smoke he could see Mullah Badreddoza running away. He could not summon a single sound to his throat to call

Badreddoza back. He understood that this shrine was actually Alladin's amazing lamp and that the Tong Khadim was the genie of the shrine. An extraordinary jinn bore him back to the corpse he had left behind in his village, the prayers for its burial and funeral completely unknown to him.

He realized, quite suddenly, that he was flanked by two men who probably did not belong to this world. Were they Munkar and Nakeer then, the angels who appeared after death to ask 'Who is your lord, what is your religion, and what is the name of your messenger?'

But these two looked familiar. They were dressed in glittering robes embroidered with gold and silver, but their faces were indistinct. One of these two mysterious figures said, 'Come with us German Mian, we'll walk you home along the railway line. We'll take you close to your home. You know don't you, that Kana had killed herself on the rail tracks exactly halfway between the shrine and home. Thieves and robbers take advantage of this incident to scare people at the spot. Travelers assume Kana's spirit still resides there. Those thieves even rob people of their clothes when they're alone. Once we take you as far as the gum tree by the railway line, you can go home safely by yourself.'

German Mian awoke under a faint beam of sunlight, accompanied by a pleasant breeze. But how strange, he was in his own bed! The south-facing window was open, letting in air. It soothed his soul. Looking around, he found himself surrounded by people – Zulfiqar Mian, Mullah Badreddoza and several other men. German Husain tried to grasp how so many people had turned up so early in the morning, and why.

Before he could ask why Badreddoza had abandoned him at the shrine the previous day, owing to which he could not return home because of his grievous injury, Bade Mullah said humbly:

'Forgive me, Mian. It wasn't my fault. We went to the shrine at Hamidhaati at the hour during which jinns visit the graves. I met them when I went into the graveyard at that time by mistake. It'll take half the day to tell you the whole story. Let me tell you briefly. Just like people, jinns too are good and evil. You'll never know what an evil jinn is like unless one of them targets you. I ran away when I saw the flaming red eyes of just such a jinn. Every man fears for his life, doesn't he, Zulfiqar Bhai?'

Zulfiqar Mian did not respond.

German Mian could not accept the fact that he would not have returned home had it not been for those two mysterious figures dressed in embroidered robes or something. Zulfiqar Mian said, 'You can't break down like this, Mian. There was a thunderstorm last night. Karim Sahib and Roychowdhury babu found you by the railway line and brought you home. Can you imagine what might have happened if they hadn't spotted you? You'd better get out of bed now and have breakfast. They will be here at around nine or ten to see how you are.'

German Mian had heard a great deal about Rezaul Karim

and Saroj Roychowdhury. They taught at the Salar National School. It was a renowned school. Anyone associated with it was viewed with awe and respect in the district. Karim Sahib belonged to Birbhum district where German Mian had come from. He had been jailed as a student twenty or twenty-five years ago. He had been agitating against the British government since his days at St Xavier's College. People deferred to someone like him, for he had been to jail. The local Congress leader Syed Maqsudal Hussain had brought them here so that an English-medium school could be set up in Salar instead of a madrasa. These nationalist teachers taught their students many things in addition to what was in their textbooks, which was precisely what some people did not approve of. They had even said 'Our boys are sent to school to study, why are the teachers brainwashing their young heads against the government?'

Rezaul Karim was a teacher of English, which he taught marvelously. He took children from poor families into the school and taught them different things after classes were done. Saroj Roychowdhury taught Bengali in the same school. He had earned a name for himself as a writer. He lived in the neighbouring village, Malihati. German Mian had also met two other teachers from the same school, Ishwar Kundu and Ramanimohan Das, but he had not heard anyone else being spoken of as much – for good or for bad – as Karim Sahib.

The Mullah-e-Sharif of the huge madrasa near the stable for elephants in Salar was Khondkar Abdul Majid. Everyone referred to him as Majid Mullah. It seemed he wanted Arabic and Farsi to be studied more extensively. It was his wish – that Hindus and Muslims from distant places should come here to learn those languages. Majid Mullah's forefathers had arrived here along with the Chowdhurys who were zamindars of Natore, to run the madrasa. But now Maqsudal Hussain, Rezaul Karim and their cohorts were luring the students away from the madrasa to their own school with the promise of teaching them English. So Majid Mullah was no longer on cordial terms with Karim Sahib and his friends.

When German Mian appeared in the front room after breakfast, Badreddoza ushered in two gentlemen. German Mian realized that these were Rezaul Karim and Saroj Roychowdhury. They were offered chairs, and fragrant drinks and salvers of paan were brought out to welcome them.

'How are you feeling now?' German Mian felt a little embarrassed in Karim Sahib's presence. To change the subject, he asked Saroj Roychowdhury, 'Written anything new, Saroj-babu?'

Saroj Roychowdhury said, 'You mean you've read my stories? I'll tell you about my new stories another day. Today let's talk about the work at hand. I believe you're an educated man – you know Arabic well. Will you teach at our school?'

German Mian was startled by this proposal. He had no conventional degree that could enable him to be a schoolmaster. But he knew English, Bengali, Arabic and Farsi equally well. He had learnt them at home, with his own efforts. Assuming that these guests would be disappointed if he said he had no wish to teach he told them, 'Why don't we keep that for another day too, Chowdhury-babu, just like your new stories? What's your opinion of the new government? Surely the League will run the administration well, don't you think?'

'What do you suppose Mian! Can the League ever provide a good government? Bengal's Muslims have voted for them because they want the formation of Pakistan. We were against the idea of separate elections on the basis of religion. Unless we can extricate ourselves from the strategies of the British, there will be riots again, Mian. We haven't learnt our lesson from the first one,' answered Karim Sahib on Saroj-babu's behalf. German Mian said, 'But you aren't neutral. You're screaming yourself hoarse for Hindustan although you know it is a transgression for Muslims to say Vande Mataram, you're saying just that. What is this Karim Sahib? Don't you think your action is against the Sharia? You're a highly educated man, what do you say?'

Rezaul Karim smiled; a single statement emerged from the smile, 'Habul watan, minal iman. Nationalism is a part of Islam and a pillar of our faith. I am fighting for my country. If the name of my country is Hindustan, it is my duty to fight for it. We are fighting for our land, the land from which Allah gave birth to us and if it's Vande Mataram that you're referring to then listen to this.

You must have heard of a country named Jordan. It is referred to as Al Urdun in Arabic. The people of this country have waged a battle to secure their independence. Muslims and non-Muslims alike are singing for King Abdullah, Asha-al-malik – long live the king, he reigns supreme. What do you have to say to that, German Sahib? That's their national anthem. Don't sing the Vande Mataram if you don't wish to; there's no compulsion. The sacred lord has said, if I had wanted to order you to prostrate yourself before anyone else but me, it would only have been your mother. Is the motherland not our mother too?'

German Mian was enraged. He had refuted Karim Sahib's illogical argument already, there was no need to dwell on it further. If Allah had desired it, he would have asked people to prostrate themselves for their mother – where did it say all this? And even if it did it was obvious that prostrating oneself in front of one's mother was an act of profanity for Allah had given no such orders.

Normally he couldn't speak when he was angry. There was no knowing what he might say in a fit of temper. Islam didn't consider it legitimate to speak in anger; no one should speak until they had brought their rage under control. Of course it was different when it came to righteous anger which was different from ordinary rage. Considering how angry he was right now it would be best for him to remain silent. Habul watan was a fake Haadith. There were many such fakes everywhere. People chanted them for their own convenience. Did Karim Sahib have any idea who among the Sahabah, the Prophet's companions, had pronounced this Haadith and when? Even the ones referred to as the Sahi Haadith had different strengths

– some of them were powerful and others were weak. It was because people like Karim Sahib said all the wrong things that their school was being wound up. He had received confirmed news about that from Majid Mollah. How could it be possible to attack madrasas and not get into trouble with Khudataala? German Mian had even heard that the Congress was sending Rezaul Karim to Baharampur. He would now have to spin thread all day. This was practically a punishment. What crime had he committed for the Congress to treat him this way? But they probably did not know yet about the school being closed down, for they would not have come looking for a teacher otherwise.

Mullah Badredduza entered holding a sheet of green paper. Agitated, he asked Karim Sahib 'what's all this, Mian? Are the Congress and the Hindu Mahasabha going to join hands to drive Muslims out? Muslims are not even being allowed to make ceremonial sacrifices today. See what it says here!' Bade Mullah began reading aloud from the paper in his hand:

A Heartfelt Appeal

We hereby submit respectfully to sympathetic Muslim brothers that on the occasion of Bakr-Eid in the year 1352, impoverished Muslims of Khidirpur village, under Hariharpara police station in the district of Murshidabad had offered a cow as sacrifice under police supervision, as demanded by their religion. Because of this crime they have been subjected to severe chastisement and torture by the powerful Hindu zamindars of the region. This has been going on for a considerable period of time. Running out of patience, the local helpless and poor Muslims were eventually forced to resort to the judicial system. Having filed and fought a case for the sake of self-defence for the past five or six months, they are now on the verge of bankruptcy and are almost starving. On one side are enormously wealthy zamindars and on the other, uneducated, flood-struck Muslims incapable of ensuring food and clothing for themselves; it is easy to surmise which way the balance tilts. Needless to say, the impoverished cannot afford litigation.

Will you abandon them in this predicament? Do you realize what they will do at this critical juncture? Will you take on their burden and share it amongst yourselves? All of you have been tested many times on these subjects; each time your response has exceeded all expectations. It is hoped that this time too, you will respond for the sake of Islam, for the sake of humanism, with financial support in consonance with your capabilities, in order to protect your beleaguered and impoverished brothers and earn infinite grace. There is no doubt that your collective participation in such a task and mission will be a shining example on the road that leads to the lord.

The Haadith Sharif says, *Man ahya sunnati 'inda fasadi ummati falahu ajru mi'ati shahid* – that is to say, Hazrat Mohammad Rasulullah has said that the man who revives the sunnah, the way of life that Muslims should follow at a time when people are deserting it will get the reward due to a hundred martyrs.

Baishakh 1, 1353

Here is my appeal, oh so humble
Help poor Muslims in deep trouble
Tarry no more, it's time to start
Donate money with a generous heart

MSH Maulabux Nadvi
Mohah Tabarak Ullah
The Royal Printing Press, Bhabta

Zulfiqar Mian appeared suddenly as Badreddoza finished reading. He couldn't have gone home – he must have been lurking nearby. He sat down in a corner of the room. Taking a one-rupee note out of his pocket, Saroj-babu gave it to Bade Mian and said, 'Here's my contribution.'

Karim Sahib laughed. Still laughing, he told German Mian, 'I realize that you consider the Habul watan minal iman a weak haadith. What I think is that this one is quite feeble too. Never mind all that, let us know whether you're willing to teach in our school. We have no teacher for Arabic at the National School. We're going now. Be well and take care.'

Zulfiqar Mian escorted them out through the front door. Returning, he whispered to German Mian, 'Will you teach at their school?'

'No,' replied German Mian.

Bade Mullah was still furious. 'That damned zamindar is a Congressman!' he exclaimed.

The process of forming Bengal's new council of ministers

was complete. There were 'Khanbahadurs' galore in prime minister Hussain Shahid Suhrawardy's cabinet, as expected. Low-born Muslims did not dare join politics. The British government had at one time given brave Muslim heroes the title of 'Khanbahadur', in return for which they had accepted subservience to their British masters. Some people still used the title earned by their fathers or grandfathers. A few though had earned it themselves. German Mian was not brave – the less said of his heroism the better – but he too hankered for a title like 'Khanbahadur'. His name would have sounded so striking – Khanbahadur German Hussain. Musing over all this, he began to taunt Zulfiqar Mian. 'Tell me Janab-e-Ala you're a Turkish dancer; I'm told the British government is handing out Khanbahadur titles for whirling dances. Why don't you apply?'

Zulfiqar Mian said, 'Don't joke about the Khanbahadur title. Do you know that Bengal's finance minister is Khanbahadur Mohammad Ali and the education minister is Khanbahadur Syed Muazzemuddin Hussain? The Khan surname implies a person is Turkish. Are there any brave people in the world besides Turks?'

German Mian chuckled. 'Turks have claimed all the good qualities I see. We only need to open a history book to know that there is no end to the wonders of your country. You needn't provide a list janab. I'm thinking of something else. The other day I saw in the gazette that our Bharatpur police station has the largest number of high schools out of all seventeen police stations in Murshidabad district – as many as nine. Even the Baharampur town police station has only six. The others have even fewer – three, two and even one in some places. Syed Muazzemuddin Hussain had hardly become the education minister when he wanted to close down the National School in Salar. No matter how much we claim that the school is being wound up because it tried to undermine the madrasa, that's not the real reason. There's something wrong somewhere. We need to talk to the mayor, Zakeria Sahib. There's a serious conspiracy going on.'

Zulfiqar Mian said, 'Forget about the conspiracy Mian Sahib, listen to me. There are three Hindus among the ministers and two of them are Namashudras, of low caste. The government would lose face otherwise. Imagine a Muslim League government to begin with, where all the important portfolios are under the control of Muslims. Heh heh heh. They have made Jogen Mandal, a Namashudra, the law minister. Heh heh heh... Lawn minister would be better.'

German Mian began spinning a yarn. 'Look, Zulfiqar Bhai it was wise of Suhrawardy to make Jogen Mandal the law minister. You know why? Suhrawardy himself is an expert in law. He has many tricks up his sleeve. Here's a Polish woman – a Russian citizen who got married in Germany to a man who lives in England. Just imagine how well he must know the law to have her convert to Islam at Nakhoda masjid and secure a divorce. Vera Khatoon becomes Bibi Noorjahan. Just like Mughal Emperor Jehangir's wife, and then he marries her too. A real chip off the old block. The father was a high court judge, Zahid Sahib. Suhrawardy practised at the Calcutta High Court for many years after getting a degree in law from Oxford. What will Jogen Mandal achieve as law minister? Nothing. Let there be a couple of Hindu names – it's good to have them. The Hindus will feel secure at the thought that their people are also a part of the Muslim League government.'

Zulfikar Ali stopped giggling and broke into peals of laughter, but Badreddoza said nothing. Perhaps he was furious because Muslims were not being allowed to sacrifice cows. German Mian was annoyed by Zulfikar Ali's chortling. Such laughter irritated him. Taking off his kurta, he said 'this game of communalism has been going on since time immemorial. It is being played now and it will be played again. On the surface the Congress thinks that Muslims are its friend. Tell me are Jawaharlal Nehru and Jinnah great friends? Then why should there be torrents of love flowing between ordinary Muslims and the Congress? What nonsense!'

Zulfiqar Mian stopped laughing. 'Do you know what Hari pandit said the other day?' he said grimly.

'What did he say?'

'He said Nehru is like Dhritarashtra. Blind and willing to do anything for power. How else could his own brother Pandu...'

German Mian interrupted Zulfiqar Mian. 'Pandu was not Dhritarashtra's own brother. They had different mothers. Vyasdev might have been their father, but their mothers were sisters. It is a sin for Muslims to marry two sisters. Never mind, go on.'

'That Pandu…'

'Who's Pandu?'

'Netaji Subhash Bose, whom they exiled. There is no sign of him anymore.'

German Mian tried in vain to gauge the extent to which the desire for power could go. Hari Pandit was right. Jawaharlal's love for power had reached a dangerous level. The Mahabharata could be enacted right here. All the characters were present. Jinnah would suit the role of Karna very well.

Fumbling in his bag, Zulfiqar Mian pulled out a paper packet and handed it to German Mian, saying, 'My wife has sent this for yours. Her fate holds no children for her. She had meant to visit your wife at her shaad ceremony, but you have not invited us. She had bought this sari, genuine silk – we got it from Saidabad.'

German Mian had heard a great deal about Saidabad, although he couldn't remember the context, so he asked Zulfiqar Mian 'Is Saidabad a famous place, Mian? I seem to have heard of it somewhere.'

'Yes, that was where the Armenians had built their silk mill. People go to Saidabad to visit their graves. Just imagine, people actually visit graves. The Dutch, the British, the French, the Portuguese, Kashmiris, Gujaratis, Iranians, Turks – all of them were involved in the silk trade in this district. My uncle's father-in-law became very rich trading in silk.'

'Horses, silk – your uncle is very fortunate, I must say. Where did the Dutch and the French set up their silk mills, Mian?'

'Not my uncle Janab, his father-in-law. Pay attention. Outsiders have been coming into Murshidabad to trade in silk from the time of Akbar. If you went to Kalikapur you'd see a huge Dutch cemetery there. Because of the wrath of Allah, all of them died there, all those silk traders. They couldn't even be buried beneath the soil of their own land. Kashimbazar is full of French graves; that's where they had set up their death mill. The Portuguese in Amanganj and Farasdanga, the Iranians in Maresoubazar, the Turks in Beldanga and the Kashmiris and Gujaratis, here and there.'

'So Mian Bhai now they only sell towels in Beldanga? Are the Turks trading in towels now? Some in jaggery and some in towels?' asked German Mian with a sardonic smile. It had become a habit with him to tease Zulfikar Mian about his Turkish antecedents. On his part Zulkiqar Mian had realized this only too well. Whether it was because of his Turkish blood or his friendship with German Mian's brother he was no longer enraged by this. On the contrary, he was amused. It was with amusement that the history-loving Zulfiqar Ali told German Mian 'What can we do? If I being Turkish can be a jaggery trader, what's wrong with towels? You can check for similarities between towels and jaggery – you're a dreamer, after all. You may well find something they have in common. But think of our fate. There we were, living in a beautiful

European country like Turkey, and now here we are in Salar, where the Pathans live. That too with you.'

A surprised German Mian said, 'When did Salar become home to Pathans? Shah Rustam's ancestors were from Arabia, weren't they?'

'Salar existed even before Shah Rustam. Salar is a line of the Jadoon tribe. The word is neither Urdu nor Farsi nor Arabic – It's Pashto. The Jadoons are the largest Pathan tribe. They used to live in Jalalabad, Khyber, Swabi, Abbotabad and Haripur. One particular group arrived here, driven out from wherever they went. Those who came were members of the first sub-tribe of Jadoons – the Salars. That's how this area got its name Mian. But there were two other sub-tribes of the Jadoons – Mansoors and Hassazais. If you went north on the train from Salar station, after Malihati and Teya, you'll come to the halt for Mian village. Many members of the Jadoon tribe still live there. How we've drifted from what we were talking about! The weaver spun his silk till magic ruined his ilk!'

It was true – there were new things to be learnt everywhere. How little we knew. German Mian thought about all that Zulfiqar Mian had told him. Maybe there were similar stories about his own village. People in the villages forgot their ancestors within three or four generations in the natural course of things. These very people had ruled over the villages once, built mosques, dug numerous lakes, but human beings were so ungrateful that they did not remember. No one wrote down anything – they weren't kings, after all. So the original people vanished from memory after a few generations.

'Silk is made from silkworms, isn't it?' said German Mian to Zulfiqar Mian. 'How strange!'

Zulfiqar Mian smiled. 'What's so strange about it, sahib?' he said. 'Your head would start reeling if you knew of all the things that Allahtaala has made in this world. Did you know that it's utterly dry inside rocks, not a drop of water, and yet there's life within? Whereas we gasp if we have to pass a day without water. Just imagine the number of people who died at Karbala by the Euphrates because of lack of water, so many of Hussain's followers! Now look how far we've drifted again – from silk to Jadoons and now to the war by the Euphrates. We could pass the entire day this way. I'd better go. Don't forget to give the sari to your wife. Don't give it to anyone else!

Zulfiqar Mian left. German Mian wondered whom he had referred to when telling him not to give the sari to anyone but his wife. Did he know magic? The magic that extracted silk from silkworms. How mysterious the sacred lord had made this world. Silk threads came from those insects' saliva, or was it their vomit? The threads were woven into cloth that people wore when they read the namaz. Think of the number of medicines made from honey, which was the vomit of bees. He had heard that even snake venom was used to manufacture medicines. How strange this world was, so full of magic!

German Mian usually took a short nap after lunch. It was an old habit of his. But he had never imagined he would have such a dream during the day. Some people said that daytime dreams were replete with illusions. He saw the two mysterious figures clearly. Instead of glittering, embroidered robes, they were dressed in silk tunics. Silkworms were weaving silk thread with their saliva all over their bodies, but German Mian could not say whether it was like the web spun by a spider or like a spider caught in a web. A pair of mysterious figures indefatigably performed magic, where white pigeons emerged from the bodies of the silkworms which then turned into flags. Then they pulled pigeons out of leaping flames too, the wings of the birds radiating light. In this light German Mian could see two faces, and as the faces grew clearer in the light they turned out to be those of prime minister Suhrawardy and Lieutenant Governor John Burrows. In front of them lay a corpse, which kept increasing in length.

Kamrunnesa gave birth to her second child that same day. It was another daughter. She was named Shanti – peace. Kamrunnesa chose the name herself. German Mian gave the child her formal name, Jahanara Banu.

~ Dar-ul-Akhira ~

THE OTHER WORLD

A nephew of Kamrunnesa's had turned up a few days before and had been admitted to the Fazil course of the madrasa at Salar. His name was Khairul Islam, but everyone called him Khoka. Even at the age of seventeen or eighteen he appeared dull and unaware of things. There was no school in his village, and he didn't want to go to the school in a nearby village because it involved a long walk. His education had all but come to a halt, which was why his father and uncle had dispatched him to German Mian's house. Kamrunnesa had absolutely no contact with her own family, yet they had quite nonchalantly sent her nephew over to get an education. Why blame the boy? He diligently ate four meals a day and steered clear of studies. Effectively, all he did was waste his time. His one shortcoming was his penchant for participating in the conversations grown-ups were having around him and insisting on having the last word. The closing statements he made were much like the prophecies of an astrologer pronounced with tremendous gravity.

Zahura was older now and was going to school too, a primary school very close to the house where boys and girls studied together. Khoka bossed Zahura around all the time as though he had taken on the mantle of being her guardian. German Mian's elder brother sent over the daily necessities, including food and fuel, at regular intervals. Tentuli brought it all in a bullock-cart. Sometimes German Mian's brother came himself to hand over some money; he was planning to buy some land hereabouts. German Mian observed that in the intervening period his brother had changed. It was obvious from the way he spoke that his views were different now. The other day he was saying that the Congress and the Hindu Mahasabha were two sides of the same dirt. A formidable Congress supporter speaking like this was surprising. Imagine someone who couldn't tolerate the slightest criticism of the Congress talking this way!

German Mian thought every day about the corpse he had seen back in the village. He didn't dare ask anyone about it. He could bring it up with his brother but he didn't have the courage to; he had always feared his brother like death itself. Was his brother connected to this corpse in any way? Was that why German Mian was unable to talk about it? He tried to ask Tentuli, but Tentuli denied everything. Sometimes he said, 'I didn't see anything.' At other times he appeared stunned at the mention of the corpse and screamed, 'You're dreaming the whole thing Mianbhai!' German Mian didn't ask Kamrennusa any questions about the corpse. What could she do after all, since she hadn't seen or heard anything; there was no point in involving her. These days Khoka had taken to blurting out every now and then, 'Riots are inevitable, no one will survive.' German Mian couldn't dismiss what the boy was saying. Was the corpse going to become a pretext for severe violence to erupt across the land? Who knew?

The World War was about to end. This was the second one. German Mian did not remember the First World War but he was closely connected with it. His father had died before he was born; German Mian did not have the good fortune of setting eyes on his father. The Prophet's father too, had died before the Prophet was born. It was strange when you thought of it – how could a person grow up without a father? In Jahura's case he couldn't even think of himself as being absent. German Mian had heard from his mother that wars were raging all over the world when he was born. The Arab countries were on the brink of one too. A man named Sharif Husain Bin Ali from Arabia began a war to secure freedom from Turkish rule. The revolution was conducted in the form of lethal guerrilla warfare. Bengal's educated Muslims had not accepted this war and had opposed Sharif Husain. German Mian's mother was fluent in Urdu and Arabic. She used to revere the Caliph of Turkey. Who else would unite the Muslims of the world? Now even the Arabs were at war to free themselves from the yoke of the Caliph, the king of Turkey. They wanted to establish their own kingdom from Syria on one side to Yemen on the other. Germany had lent support to the king of Turkey. The

Muslims of Bengal realized that Germany alone was their true friend. And that was why German Mian's mother had chosen this name for her son as a mark of respect and gratitude to that country. Whenever German Mian tried to tell Khoka stories of the First World War, he said, 'I don't like hearing about battles and killing, fufajan. Tell me stories about nymphs. But riots are inevitable, no one will survive.'

German Mian began telling Khoka the story of the nymphs in Gul-e-baqabli. It was one of his favourites. He loved telling the tale of Taj-ul-mulk's amazing travels. Khoka used to fall asleep as he listened to the story, but Zahura would not. She listened attentively to the entire story and asked never-ending questions. Zahura's little brain could not absorb the fact that one couldn't ask so many questions during a fairy-tale. German Mian found it difficult to cope with so many queries all by himself. His plight had arisen ever since Kamrunnesa Bibi had become busier with their younger daughter. He began to feel fatigued. Frequently, he sought out weighty tasks to avoid his household responsibilities, but his predicament did not end.

Either to rid himself of this peril or out of a sense of duty German Mian began to frequently attend the secret as well as open meetings of the Muslim League. Not that he was allowed into every clandestine gathering of the League; in fact, German Mian didn't even get to know about most of them. Still, he often visited the office of the Muslim National Guard, which had opened a branch here, and every time he went he heard how Muslims were unable to flourish amongst a Hindu majority – which was why a separate Muslim state was needed comprising the areas where the majority were Muslims. This was the formal policy of the League, and so Murshidabad would become part of Pakistan. However, the Hindus were much more powerful in the Rarh areas of Murshidabad. They were far ahead of the Muslims when it came to education. Moreover they had kept in regular touch with the Congress and the Hindu Mahasabha. No matter which party's line they toed by day, they were united at night. All of them spoke in one voice when it came to national issues, not in two, as Muslims did. The Hindus wanted to keep Murshidabad in Hindustan by hook or by crook. Meanwhile, Bapuji had said that Pakistan could be created only over his dead body. What an ungodly thing to say!

Amongst Muslims, Prime Minister Suhrawardy was a well-educated man. He was also a barrister, who could lecture flawlessly in Bengali, English and Urdu. Apparently he was learning Polish and Russian from his wife. He had said that if India were partitioned into Hindustan and Pakistan, he would have one foot in each land. To which a vivacious young man from the National Guard had responded, 'Those of us who live on the border will have a fantastic view of Suhrawardy.'

Reprimanding the soldier, Mir Naseeb Ali, the president of the local wing of the Muslim National Guard, had said, 'Suhwawardy is saying all this for the benefit of the common man. In truth he wants to create an independent Bengal and doesn't give a damn whether our Murshidabad is allotted to

Pakistan or not. He's a pimp of power – why else would he join hands with Sarat Bose, Akhil Dutta and Kiran Roy to create an independent Bengal? Neither the Muslim League nor the Congress will agree to this. Their free Bengal will never be formed and meanwhile the Muslim League has been weakened.'

A member of the audience gathered at the meeting said, 'What did Jinnah Sahib say about Murshidabad?'

'What can the son of a Ismaili Khwaja possibly say?' said Mir sahib. 'They are Shias after all, how will they understand the pain of the Sunnis?'

German Mian knew that the Muslim League's Kasem Ali Mirza was a Shia too. Was that why he was actively trying to include Murshidabad in Pakistan? His father Wasef Ali Mirza was a member of the Congress, the party to which Maulana Abul Kalam Azad, a Sunni, belonged. Now if Bengal's Muslims were going to stir up trouble amongst themselves using the Sunni-Shia divide, who could help them? For instance, Zulfiqar Mian was a Shia Alevi, while German Mian was a Sunni Hanafi, but there was no lack of love and amiability between them. Then why were these leaders and learned men trying to drive a wedge between Muslims? Maybe the dream of Pakistan would die this way. Murshidabad would get nothing at all.

Even after German Mian left the meeting, the worry niggling in his mind didn't go away. He returned home directly and instead of sitting down in the drawing room sent urgently for Badreddoza. Bringing up the issue of Jinnah, he said, 'Please fetch Zulfiqar Ali at once, bhai. I need to rid myself of my suspicions.' He was convinced that no one else could tell him the truth. Badreddoza went away, and Zulfiqar Ali appeared shortly. At once German Mian asked him 'Who are the Khwaja Ismailis?' What Zulfiqar Ali said in answer was, 'Look, Muslims have many flaws. It's impossible to list them all. The seventh of the twelve Imams whom some Shias believe in was Musa Ibn-e-Zafar. The Ismailis acknowledge Musa's brother, Ismail Ibn-e-Zafar, as an Imam. Two groups were formed over this. Both of them hold Pir Sadruddin in great reverence. Let me tell you something, but you mustn't say this to anyone else, bhai. The Muslim community in which Jinnah was born believes in the ten avatars of Vishnu. When a man dies his property is divided in the Hindu way. The Muslim League is a party of Shias, not Sunnis. I'm saying this as a Shia myself, though they might abuse me as an Alevi.'

German Mian was taken aback. Had he abandoned his forefathers' faith by quitting the Congress and joining the Muslim League? Allah, whom everyone worshipped, alone knew the answer. 'Why do you call it a party of Shias?' he asked Zulfiqar Ali.

'There are two things I have to tell you,' Zulfiqar Mian answered hastily. 'First, why is Maulana Abul Kalam Azad still with the Congress? And two, the Muslim League was started with the Aga Khan's money. Nawab Khwaja Salimullah, Nawab Mohsin Ul Mulk – which of them is a Sunni, tell me that?'

German Mian had nothing to say. He was rather surprised by

what he heard. He wondered why the Aga Khan was accepted as an Imam in that case. If Jinnah, being a Khwaja Ismaili, could accept the twelve Imams, how could he also accept the Aga Khan? He was an Ismaili Shia too, but the forty-eighth Imam. His real name was Sir Sultan Mohammad Shah. He was Aga Khan III.

Zulfiqar Mian was enraged when German Mian told him this. 'Forget all this, Mian. He is a Nizari Imam. We don't accept anyone beyond the twelve Imams. He is in hiding now and will appear at the right time to rescue us. As for the Aga Khan, he married a Russian dancer, after which he married two French women. If you have money you can do anything. You can be an Imam, you can have several white women as your wives, what can we possibly say? It's best to remain silent.'

From his conversations with Zulfiqar Mian it became clear to German Mian that 'Aga Khan' was a title. The largest sect among the Ismailis was the Nizari. The Ismailis still believed in Imams, Musa's descendants did not. To the Shias, there could be no more Imams after the first twelve. The word Aga was Turkish, meaning noble or lord. Hasan Ali Shah had established the title of Aga a long time ago. He was the forty-sixth Imam. The Aga Khan who was the forty-eighth Imam was Hasan Ali Shah's grandson. So if Jinnah Sahib believed in other Imams besides the first twelve, there was nothing that anyone could say, and these were religious matters, there was no right or wrong about them. It was all a matter of personal faith.

At this time Khoka intruded into the conversation. 'Buy me

a Jinnah-cap please, fufajan, I don't like this round cap. But riots are inevitable, no one will survive.'

'All in good time,' German Mian told Khoka. 'Run along now.' Then he made enquiries about the Ramzan moon with Zulfiqar Mian. The roza was supposed to start tomorrow or the day after. Subhanallah!

A shining star was often visible in the eastern sky these days. German Mian had a pair of Russian binoculars at home, which he had used many times to check whether the star had a tail. Just like the tails some kites had. If the star had a tail it would be a fiery one and could be easily distinguished from other stars. Several passages in the Haadith Sharif hinted at this. Besides, the month of Joishtho had seen both a solar and a lunar eclipse. The lunar eclipsc had taken place exactly a fortnight after the solar eclipse – neither of them in the month of Ramzan. This too was in the Haadith. Would He not arrive during this Ramzan either? He was meant to appear when the world was filled with sin, when humans had almost exterminated themselves fighting one another. It wasn't written clearly how long He would stay on earth. Some said it would be for seven years and others said nineteen. Somewhere in between, probably – not less than seven and not more than nineteen. When his sojourn on earth ended, Judgement Day would be upon everyone, the day of final reckoning. Once Imam Mehdi arrived everyone would hear his call; his words would reach the ears of every honest Muslim. He would appear and save Nabiji's brothers in the community. Imam Mehdi's father had died before he was born, just like Nabiji or German Mian. He would arrive on horseback, his brow wide, his nose sharp, his eyes lined with surma. Peace would not be established in this world till he came.

Khoka was not a child, yet he refused to observe the roza. Zahura was very young, but she still observed the first of the fasts. Kamrunnesa Bibi had to practically use force to discontinue fasting, but she scolded Khoka for ignoring the roza. The boy had burst into tears and told German Mian, 'My belly feels like it's on fire Fufajan. The flames turn everything to ashes. But riots are inevitable, no one will survive.'

Twenty rozas passed in the flash of an eye. Numbers twenty-one, twenty-three, twenty-five, twenty-seven and twenty-nine are especially important to Muslims. Allah's angel Gibrail had appeared to the Prophet on one of those days, and the divine revelation had been made. Through his angel, Allahtaala made the revelation to the Prophet in the form of the Quran. Before the Quran there had been the Jabur and the Injil. As the Quran was revealed in the course of the month one had to complete reading the entire book within the month. This increased the weight of one's good deeds and lessened the burden of sins. The elders said that Allahtaala granted all the fervent prayers made by such a follower. Only if the scales tipped on the side of good deeds and not of sins every day on the field of resurrection did a man go to heaven. Reading the Haadith Sharif carefully made it clear that most elders considered the twenty-seventh night as the night on which the Quran was revealed, but there was no certainty. Everyone assumed that the Quran had arrived on earth on an odd-numbered day after the twentieth. German Mian made no pretence about possessing superior knowledge. He prayed to Allahtaala for maghfirat, salvation, on every odd-numbered night. He organized lavish iftaar meals for the poor and the deprived to break their fasts in the evening on all five nights. Besides offering the namaz, he studied the Quran with greater emphasis.

On all the five days a Milad mehfil was organized in his house after the Asr namaz in the afternoon. There was a group of Muslims who did not accept this practice, terming it anti-Sharia, but those who accepted Hazrat Mohammad as the light of the light did not think that way, let alone say so. The other group of Muslims was up in arms because a qiyam or encomium addressed to Hazrat Mohammad was read out at Milad. No one suggested that Allah Tabaraktaala had any equal – it was with complete devotion to an Allah without any equal that the finest of his prophets were praised. German Mian saw nothing wrong in this. Being a Shia, Zulfiqar Mian was staunchly opposed to the Milad mehfil, which was why he never showed up. Mullah Badreddozza took care of all the arrangements single-handedly. He and German Mian treated everyone who read the namaz and observed the roza to an Iftar feast so that no one had to go home to break their fast after sundown. Twenty-one rozas went off well. On the twenty-third Ramzan, Monday, Zulfiqar Ali came to German Mian's house after the dawn namaz. He looked perturbed. What he said terrified German Mian.

The Hindu Mahasabha's Savarkar & Co. had apparently declared that they would not allow the formation of Pakistan. They had gone so far as to say they had no objection in taking up arms if need be. Moreover, they were strongly opposed to special privileges for Muslims as recommended by the Cabinet Mission. Bapuji was silent. He was naturally opposed to arms, for his non-violent movement would suffer in that case. The Hindu Mahasabha people were saying so themselves. Jinnah Sahib had added the words 'Bismillah-e-Rahman-e-Rahim', 'in the name of Allah the beneficent, the merciful', and got the members of the Muslim League to sign the proposal for the formation of Pakistan. The League was saying that a general strike had been called next Friday, the twenty-seventh day of Ramzan, to protest against the joint opposition to Muslims on the part of the Hindu Mahasabha and the Congress. Shops and offices would not be allowed to open. Would the Hindus accept this general strike? Khoka's prophecy wouldn't come true, would it? German Mian was convinced that riots were inevitable, that no one would survive. The prospect of having to witness what would happen here in Bengal three or four days before Id-ul-fitr alarmed and frightened him.

The Suhrawardy government declared Friday, the twenty-seventh day of Ramzan, a holiday. Husain Shahid Suhrawardy had kept the home ministry to himself. So while Muslims felt reassured, the Hindus did not. Early in the morning German Mian heard on the radio that the situation in Calcutta was already tense. The Hindus had opened their shops in protest against the general strike. The Muslims were trying different methods to close them down. When pleas didn't work they were using force. It was even being said that the two groups were throwing stones at each other, and several people had been injured by bricks. As the day progressed, dubious elements had hit the streets with sticks, iron rods and bombs. All of them belonged to the Muslim League, supporters of the strike.

An undercurrent of tension spread across the villages as the news from Calcutta came in. Most of the news was being suppressed on the radio. German Mian did not know where the people of the National Guard were getting their information. No one was inclined to check the veracity of the news – everyone was on edge. The National Guard was making secret preparations. If something were to happen around here, they wouldn't spare the Hindus. It was being rumored that the members of the Hindu Mahasabha were getting ready with guns and bombs too. The Hindus were outnumbered here, making them more frightened and apprehensive. The local Muslim zamindar, Kumar Keramatullah Chowdhury, had offered his support to them. He had declared to every Hindu and Muslim here that if even a single Hindu was murdered, it would be over his dead body. His private stick-wielding army was armed and ready, prepared to jump into the fray at the first command. German Mian was not in favour of killing people. It would be far better to remain under British rule than to have Pakistan born out of bloodshed and riots. Meanwhile, Kamrunnesa Bibi pointed out something that couldn't be brushed aside.

According to the proposal of the Cabinet Mission, the British government could just leave once they had handed over the administration to Indians. What was their objective behind the idea of opening up a wound? Everyone had accepted the original suggestion, not that there weren't minor problems with it, but the Hindu and Muslim leaders could have sorted all that out between themselves. Apparently it was the British who had come up with the notion of a Hindu-dominated India and a Muslim-dominated Pakistan in order to instigate the two communities to clash. But German Mian could not accept Kamrunnesa's logic in its entirety. The Muslim League was bound to demand the formation of Pakistan, and neither Jinnah nor Nehru was a child. The Congress had consistently opposed the proposal for Pakistan. That the Muslim League would call a general strike as a result was entirely expected, and even a child knew that if the League were to call a general strike the Hindus would not support it. Kamrunnesa's argument was that the British were responsible for the current situation in the country. They had not appointed an interim government when they should have, and when they finally did none of the Muslim representatives in it was a member of the League. Even German Mian accepted that this was a deep British conspiracy.

There was no Dua Durood, invocations to compliment the Prophet, or Quran Tilawat on the twenty-seventh day of Ramzan, which came only once a year, the day most replete with blessings. German Mian read the namaz perfunctorily and spent the day fretting about the riots in Calcutta. There was no Milad, he didn't even invite anyone to Iftar. For the first time in the holy month of roza, German Mian had only Kamrunnesa Bibi as his companion for Iftar. The radio was turned on, with news coming in throughout the day, but the information brought in by people was much more fraught than the news on the radio. Rumours were afloat that the riots that had started in the Beleghata area of north Calcutta had spread to Rajabajar, Sealdah, Harrison Road, Wellington Square and Corporation Street. Groups of Hindus were slaughtering Muslims, while Muslims were pouncing on any Hindus they saw. Let alone sleeping well on such a night; staying awake was difficult enough. An ancient dream floated up in German Mian's memory.

He was wandering about on fallow land, which had never been cultivated. Walking across this land, he arrived at a crossroads. Numerous roads had converged here, each of them so serpentine that it could easily be confused for a snake. He knew that violent wars had broken out on every road leading to this gigantic confluence. Much of the land on earth was being destroyed; many people were being annihilated. German Mian spotted three birds. Were these the Ababils who had pelted stones at the soldiers riding in on elephants? German Mian believed they did not belong to this world. Their shapes were like distorted maps. They took off their clothes to bathe in blood. Was this bath inevitable? German Mian had no reply to this dream. There was no one like the Prophet Yusuf to explain the meaning of his dream to him. He felt a stab of fear. There was no knowing how many victims these riots would claim. How many children would lose their fathers. How many wives their husbands. German Mian felt like weeping, but what could tears offer? Neither a solution nor an escape route. Only his vision became blurred.

Those from the village who had moved to the city for jobs had come back. Where were the ones who had not? Had they been killed in the riots? Questions like these began to hover in the air. Calcutta's Hindus were apparently claiming that Suhrawardy's police had not stepped into the Hindu areas, and Muslim hoodlums had been ordered to do whatever they liked. Murder, arson, rape – they had baulked at nothing. There had been riots in Calcutta earlier in 1926, and now, twenty years later, they were being repeated. It was obvious that the Hindus would blame the Muslim League for the riots. The responsibility for not being able to stop the riots had fallen on Suhrawardy. Husain Shahid Suhrawardy used to be a member of the Congress once, but he had quit, blaming the party for the 1926 riots. The irony was that he had been forced to turn once again to the Congress now. Suhrawardy sought Bapuji's help. His father Zahid Sahib was fighting death, with his daughters reading the Quran by his bed so that he might sleep in peace. He had not heard of the riots, for he was unconscious. The Muslims who came back from Calcutta brought plenty of news which was important not just for German Mian but for many of the supporters of the League. Instead of the traditional embrace on Eid, everyone spoke of the riots, their voices lowered.

Gopal Pantha, who belonged to a family of butchers in Bowbazar, had apparently decided to slaughter Muslims instead of goats. Two milkmen had died in the Hindu-Muslim riots in Beleghata. When they heard this, Gopal and his cronies hit the streets with daggers, bombs and pipe-guns. Gopal Pantha had informed his cohorts that they would have to kill ten Muslims for every Hindu who had been murdered. American soldiers who were stationed in Calcutta during the Second World War had apparently sold Gopal pistols and cartridges at dirt-cheap prices. Many members of the Allied troops had not yet left Calcutta after the war. Gopal Pantha was getting up to four rounds of bullets from them in exchange for a bottle of whisky.

Jugal Ghosh was another of the Hindu generals.

The leader of the Muslim National Guard, Ghulam Rasool had pleaded with Gopal Pantha, 'There's been too much killing already on both sides. We have to stop this mass slaughter now. We are not prepared to kill anymore. We are ready for a ceasefire.'

Gopal did not heed Ghulam. At Suhrawardy's request Bapuji himself had asked Gopal Pantha to throw down his arms when the riots had broken out, but Gopal had not complied with his request either. The Muslims who had come back from Calcutta were saying they could no longer live there. The neighbourhoods were inundated with Hindu ruffians. They had plenty of money which they were using to buy guns and ammunition and blow away any Muslim they saw. Muslims had no money, how many could they kill with sticks and iron rods alone? The weaker side always wanted a ceasefire – that was the rule. But why would the powerful want to stop the riots when they knew they would win?

On top of this, the Sikhs had sided with the Hindus. The Sikh leaders of Calcutta had asserted vehemently in public, 'The Muslims haven't learnt their lesson from their defeat in the 1926 riots. They've surfaced again. We will teach the Muslims a suitable lesson in the riots this time.' Four days before the riots began, Brigadier McKinley had ordered his troops, 'Everyone must remain in the barracks on Direct Action Day. No one is to go out.' The Muslims said the riots would not have erupted had their processions in Tala and Belgachhia not been obstructed. It wasn't just in Calcutta but also in Howrah where the terrible killings were going on. The Muslim louts of Howrah had apparently taken the responsibility of acting as Suhrawardy's bodyguards.

German Mian began to wonder who the bodyguards, for the millions who had returned from the famine and the World War a short while ago, would be. Suhrawardy had no fear of being killed in the riots, after all. No Hindu or Muslim leader had died, only ordinary people had. His vision blurred, he saw Imam Mehdi approaching on horseback and stopping this kotal-e-aam, this mass slaughter. But before he could make this thought settle in, he felt a churning in his stomach that frightened him to no end. Jinns and nymphs possessed the body in times of danger and their grip became stronger when one was passing stool or urine. If one went to the toilet then, the demon with the inverted ankles and elbows was bound to appear, the same one who retreated when he appeared to be approaching, who came closer and pounced when appearing to be going away. His movements lengthened the distance between them sometimes, and shortened it at other times. Just like the corpse left behind near his home in the village, which was lengthening with every passing day.

Daylight waned. The darkness made German Mian think of a gigantic bird smothering the world with its black wings. He had heard that the angel Gibrail had six hundred wings, each of which could cover the entire earth. But these were not Gibrail's wings. The one who appeared at the time of riots and killings was Malak-ul-maut, the angel of death, Azrael. German Mian felt very afraid. Here he was, smothering his urge to relieve himself, and just on his side were the wings of the angel of death. What was he to do now! Just then Badreddoza appeared, and German Mian breathed a sigh of relief.

'Would you like come with me to listen to Satya Pir's songs, Mian?' asked Badreddoza.

'Yes, I would,' said German Mian. 'But you have to do something for me first... you must come with me to the latrine. You can wait outside. Once I finish I'll come with you.' Badreddoza complied, and German Mian answered the call of nature before accompanying him to the venue. It was best to go and listen to the music, for it was comforting to be amongst people in times of trouble. Singing the songs pleased Satya Pir, and helped avert many dangers. 'What's the performance today?' asked German Mian.

'Sohrab and Rustam,' answered Badreddoza.

German Mian pictured Rustam plunging a dagger into his son Sohrab's breast. And yet they were both innocent and unknown to each other. Had Rustam known, could he ever have stabbed his own flesh and blood? Or could Sohrab have wounded his own father? He was searching for his parent whom he had never seen. And Rustam was instigated by evil people to kill his own child.

German Mian asked Badreddoza, 'You said the performance is in Mayor Zakeria's mango orchard, but aren't all of them in Calcutta where the riots are raging? How are they?'

'As you'd expect. His son-in-law is the famous barrister Syed Mehboob Murshed from Shahpur who hasn't a moment to spare. He travels all over the city all day in an Anjuman-e-Mafidul-Islam car, offering help to the riot struck.'

'Mehboob Sahib is Salek Sahib's son. Salek Sahib used to be the district magistrate. Even the British were afraid of him. It runs in their blood. His father was fearless too, always helping others. They're descendants of Imam Husain, you see. Mehboob's mother comes from an illustrious family. Salek Sahib's wife is a descendant of the war hero, Khaled Bin Waled.'

'Yes, and Salek Sahib's brother-in-law is Sher-e-Bangla Fazlul Huq.'

'Mehboob Sahib is a big-hearted man. If he doesn't come to the aid of people, who will? He's highly educated. I believe he was the first Bengali to get the first-class first rank in the bar examination of the British. There's no end to their talents. He belongs to the Kaderia gharana, and also recites Rabi Thakur's poems fluently.'

Still conversing they reached Zakeria Sahib's orchard. Chand Mohammad was singing by the light of lanterns, a flag in his hand, accompanied by Deben Chain on the dhol. Chand Mohammad sang in his sonorous voice.

Zakeria Sahib's brother Dr Abdullah was seated beneath the marquee on one side of the orchard. He had saved the entire Salar region from kala-azar. Upen Brahmachari, who had invented the vaccination for kala-azar, had died about six months ago. His medicine had eradicated kala-azar not just from this region but also from the entire country. Abdullah Sahib was a disciple of Upen Brahmachari. Everyone knew the man seated next to him under the marquee. Ustad Kader Bux. He was nearly seventy. If a nawab of Hindustani music was here at the recital of the music of Satya Pir, he must be in search of a new raga. The singer Chand Mohammad, who was playing the role of Sohrab, was lamenting about his loving mother, who lived in the distant land of Tartars. Her father, his grandfather, was the king of the enormous kingdom of Samangaon, which he ruled with an iron hand. Sohrab was desperate to see his father. He had heard his mother say that his father was the unparalleled military expert of Persia, his name struck terror in the hearts of every brave warrior in the world. But Sohrab had never set eyes on him. His father, too, had not bothered to visit his child under the impression that he had had a daughter. Was Sohrab to pay for this father's sins? Chand Mohammad sang in Sohrab's voice.

Would Sohrab ever be united with his father Rustam, general of King Kay Kavus? People were saying that the king and his general were at loggerheads. Rustam was not prepared to go to war for Persia anymore. How was Sohrab to meet his father if the general did not come to the battlefield? And if he did not pick up his sword, defeat was inevitable for King Kay Kavus. Sohrab would decimate the army of Persia with his Tartar troops.

Now Iran's soldiers began to appear on the battlefield. Sohrab's probing eyes sought Rustam. They would meet today. After this, Sohrab wished to pay his respects to his grandfather, Jal. His white-haired grandfather had been abandoned by his father Shaam in the Alburz mountain in the belief that he was the child of a demon. An enormous eagle had saved his life. The amulet that Sohrab's mother had tied around his arm had been given to her before his birth by his father Rustam. The amulet held an image of the eagle, his grandfather's savior, which would enable Rustam to recognize him at once.

The battlefield was bedecked. All the arrangements for battle had been made. The deerskin-clad Tartar soldiers were carrying long spears. Cavalries from Turkey, Ferghana and Casbin had arrived. Troops from Bokhara, Khiva and Khorassan were rampaging over the battlefield. Only Rustam was nowhere to be seen. Engaged in a dispute with the king, he had refused to fight. King Kay Kavus took off his crown and placed it at Rustam's feet. His ire appeased, Rustum appeared on the battlefield.

Although Rustam joined the battle, he kept his identity a secret from Sohrab, who would not have fought had he known his father was there. The stratagem of the kings of Iran and of Tartar resulted in a pitched battle between father and son. Both the kings knew that neither of them would fight if their real identities were revealed, and both kings were confident of their own victory. Father and son faced one another. The young Sohrab was far superior to the ageing Rustam in the art of battle. But, despite numerous opportunities, he did not slay Rustum. Something held him back, forcing him to say, my heart says you are Rustum. Upon the lord tell me if this is so, for then there shall be no more play-acting of war.

Rustam seized the opportunity and flung Sohrab to the ground, planting himself on his chest. Drawing his sharp dagger he plunged it into Sohrab's breast without caring for the protocol of warfare. Laughing like a ghoul, he said, 'Had enough of war Tartar? You had thought you would plunder Iran's wealth and present it to Afrasiab? That the sight of my head severed from my body would make all of Persia sing your praises out of fear? That Iran would crumple at a Tartar's feet?' Sohrab was at death's door. He declared, 'When my father Rustam comes to hear of this unjust war, your last day will also be nigh.' Taking off his amulet, he handed it to Rustam, who stared at the image of the eagle on it, bewildered.

For a moment, he stood stock-still, like a tree struck by lightning. The next moment he slumped unconscious to the ground muttering, I am an unfortunate father.

Tears streamed down German Mian's cheeks as he listened to the singer Chand Mohammad's description of the final hours of the father and son's lives. Badreddoza wiped his eyes with his sleeve. Both of them would go home now. The play was over.

German Mian was reminded of his own village. Why had he moved to this luckless land? Was it just to live in Pakistan? But there was no assurance that his hope would be fulfilled. It wasn't clear why the tragedy of the play had become his own. Chand Mohammad's voice kept ringing in his ears.

~ Al-Jannah ~

PARADISE

Believe in your dreams. The entrance to the eternal world is concealed in them.

A year had passed since the riots in Calcutta. The orgy of killing had begun on the twenty-seventh day of Ramzan in the Hijri year of 1365. The rioting continued for several days, and secret clashes continued even after the official announcement that it had ended. It would be wrong to say that the heat was not being felt here in Murshidabad district. Many of the people who worked at the bakery or the leather factory had either died or disappeared. Most had returned to the village, however. German Mian was astonished by those who had survived the famine, the war, and the riots. Some of them were waiting for Pakistan to be born, their dreams clutched to their hearts. Not everyone, though. Many were starving – to toss a proposal for the formation of Pakistan at them was to mock them.

Hafiz Molla was a renowned landowner in these parts; his case was different. All of his property was in Murshidabad district. Even though he lived right at the border of Burdwan, he had no land in that district. He didn't care for politics, believing that Pakistan was for Muslims and Hindustan for Hindus. He had long harboured the desire to buy land owned by the Hindus in the neighbouring village of Harinya to increase his holdings. But why would they sell the land on which their homes stood, or the land they farmed? Hafiz Molla had sniffed out an opportunity. If Murshidabad became part of Pakistan, these buggers would have to sell all their possessions and flee. He could not contain his delight at the prospect of buying so much land dirt cheap. He strutted about all day twirling his moustache and fingering his beard, injecting his enthusiasm into the social gatherings in the village. Word had spread that the Nagen Pandits, Rabi Bamuns and Binu Kayets, all Hindus, would no longer remain in Harinya. Their Muslim sharecroppers and farmhands were floating rumours. Apparently it was almost settled that they would move five miles away to Agardanga in Burdwan district. Aman Kazi, Arab Sheikh and other Muslims had sent proposals for swapping land. But Aman Kazi or Arab Sheikh would not be able to take the entire land, for they did not have enough for a full exchange. The Hindus of Agardanga would not move to Harinya. When all this became public knowledge, Hafiz Molla began secret confabulations with Nagen Pandit and the others. Not stopping there, he also sent word to Aman Kazi and the rest that when they moved to Harinya it would be difficult for them to live in houses that had Hindu shrines. They would have to light candles at the shrines every day, or else danger would befall them and the house would be infested by jinns and spirits. On the other hand, lighting candles would bring dishonor to the religion of their forefathers. Hafiz Mian wanted the Hindus of Harinya to sell all their property to him and leave. Everyone knew that Murshidabad would be allotted to Pakistan. The official announcement would be made on the night of the twenty-seventh of Ramzan, exactly a year after the Calcutta riots.

Ramzan arrived in no time. The night of this roza was called Laylatul qadr. On this night Muslims would be freed from British rule, and Pakistan would be founded. Hindustan would get its independence a day later. Murshidabad had been allocated to Pakistan. German Mian did not know what independence was. All he knew was that Jordan, Lebanon and Syria had been freed from British rule the year before. Pakistan would be created on the night of Laylatul qadr – by the infinite grace of Khudataala. The night was also known as Shab-e-qadr. Angels descended in large groups to earth on this night to watch the Ibadat Bandagi, the display of devotion, by human beings. When Allahtaala had created human beings, these angels had asked, 'Why are you creating humans, Lord? For they will only wreak havoc upon the world, they will kill people.' Now the same angels would watch the flag of Pakistan fluttering over the world on this night of destiny. From the first hour of darkness to the last, they would alight on earth, offering their salutations to the untiring devout. Had any country in the world been created on the night of Shab-e-qadr? Pakistan would be the first. And Murshidabad would become part of this sacred land on this holy night. A strange thrill ran through German Mian. He opened his book to read what had ensued on the Shab-e-qadr.

It was a night when fortunes would be written, when fate would be plunged into crisis.

This was the night when the destiny of the entire world, of all of humanity, would change, and it was this night upon which Allahtaala had blessed with success the creation of the new country. Who knew whether this was good, or as the learned men of the Deoband were predicting, the new country would become a laboratory of England and Russia. German Mian read:

'Even if the decision is taken to annihilate a nation, it will be for the betterment of all humanity.'

He opened the Quran Sharif and began to read the surah, the chapter, that had been composed for this special night:

'It has been revealed to us on the Shab-e-qadr, the night of destiny.
Do you know what the night of destiny is?
The night is finer than a thousand months.
With permission granted by the command of the lord, angels and Rooh-al-ameen, or Jibreel, descend on this night.
This night is one of complete peace and security – until dawn.'

German Mian went on to read the twelve rakats of the namaz of Shab-e-qadr before settling down to his prayers.

Then he retired to his room with his radio. He had named his room the khwabghar, the chamber of dreams. He knew, as Allahpak had declared, that prayers were preferable to sleep on this night. Yet he switched on the radio, for he simply had to listen to the news about the formation of Pakistan. But – how annoying! – the radio had to choose this day of all days to break down. He didn't know what to do. German Mian went to bed earlier than usual during the month of fasting because he had to eat his sehri early in the morning before the sun rose. Tonight, too, his body yearned to sleep. But before he could drift into slumber, a voice floated up in the darkness, a familiar voice.

'I am Jul, the badshah of jinns. I have a plea for you, huzoor.'

German Mian felt the onset of fear. Why was Jul Jenahen here again? King Suleiman had killed his son Baalzebul, who had been acting like the devil. This badshah of jinns had already approached German Mian with a proposal for marriage to Lucifa, daughter of Baalzebul. German Mian had neither accepted nor declined. Was the badshah of jinns going to repeat his proposal? An irked German Mian was forced to speak: 'Don't expect me to marry her. I have a wife…children too. If she gets to know she will kill me.'

'I know you're married already. That's not what I'm here to talk about now.'

German Mian screamed in Hindi, 'I have no desire to hear what your problem is.'

Jul Jenahen said meekly, 'Lucifa is my granddaughter. You don't have to marry her. Just let her stay with you. She wants to live in Pakistan, janab. Sharifabad has laid claim to this Fateh Singh subdivision that you live in. Lucifa wants to live in this country, please allow her to stay with you.'

German Mian was in a quandary. He had planned to bring up the subject of a horse when he met Jul Jenahen, badshah of jinns. Jinns knew a lot about horses. They could pick horses well; spot the most spirited stallions straight away. Arab horses were sold at the market at Tangramari in this district. Horses from Sherpur and camels from Tangramari, went the legend. But if he were to ask this pest for help, the jinn would seize the opportunity and saddle German Mian with his granddaughter. No, it was best not to tell him anything. Had he read German Mian's mind? Some jinns were mind-readers. The badshah of jinns continued, 'Do you know why no one wants their daughter to be married to a family from this Fateh Singh area? People from this locality are very rude. But then the poor want their daughters to be married to someone here because people here don't lack for food and clothing. Do you know that?

'You'll get your horse, don't worry, and I'll bring you a camel too for you to sacrifice. Do you know Mian, the king of Cossim bazar has been roundly defeated by Harun Rashid Digar in a court case. The litigation was over the market at Beldanga. But how was the king of Cossim bazar to contend with Harun Sahib, who had the jinns on his side. They played such havoc with the documents that the king was crushed.

Remember no one can defeat those who have the support of the jinns. Every trouble, every difficulty is eliminated from their lives. I shall leave now. I'll be back in your service soon. Don't forget what I said about Lucifa.'

German Mian snapped out of the no-man's land between sleep and wakefulness. He got out of bed. It wasn't as though he wasn't afraid any more, but his fear from the first encounter with the badshah of the jinns had largely disappeared. Feeling very thirsty, he had a drink of water. It was late, well past midnight. The announcement of the formation of Pakistan was to have been made at midnight. If that were the case, this was his first drink of water on Pakistan's soil. Even when he had slaked his thirst, he had no inclination to go back to bed, for if he slept now, he would be unable to wake up at dawn to have his sehri. The roza would lose its strength if he skipped the meal. It was the night of the twenty-seventh of Ramzan; the day that would follow would have the same date. For Muslims, the date changed every evening. The new day began at sunset, lasting till the sun set the next day. Unlike Christians, faithful Muslims did not consider the hour of midnight as the beginning of a new day. Hindus considered sunrise the start of the day. Pakistan's journey had begun on this Ramzan. Who chose such a beautiful name for the country? German Mian had heard the story from Chowdhury Rahmat Ali. The P of Punjab, A of the Afghan area, K of Kashmir, the E of east Bengal, the S of the Sindhu province and the 'Tan' of Baluchistan – all these added up to the dream country of Pak-e-stan, or Pakistan. The name meant 'sacred land'. Murshidabad had been given to east Bengal. Therefore he was now an inhabitant of Pakistan. The date of the twenty-seventh of Ramzan, 1366 Hirji, would be written in letters of gold.

German Mian felt a thrill similar to the one he had experienced on seeing the two strange people in the village and the woman behind purdah. Kamrunnesa Bibi had given birth to a second child some time ago. This innocent child was now a citizen of Pakistan. How infinite Allahtaala's compassion was – the baby had belonged to Hindustan in her mother's womb, but by the time she became aware of her surroundings she belonged to Pakistan. Kamrunnesa had named her well – Shanti, for peace.

German Mian had not been happy at all since leaving Birbhum. Peace and comfort had disappeared from his life. Now whether it was because of the birth of Shanti or the company of Zulfiqar Mian, Badreddoza and several others, he felt the same sense of calm that had allowed him to settle down here in Murshidabad. Along with all this there had been the dream of Pakistan, and the fulfillment of that dream had brought him peace too. Leaving aside the capital of Murshidabad, Salar was the most cultured area in the district. That was why the place was named Sarkar Sharifabad. On top of this it was part of the renowned Fateh Singh subdivision. Other people in the district were in awe of it. This was the place German Mian had made his home.

German Mian had heard that humans had apparently had

tails once. People with a western education said as much. Nauzubillah, forgive me, Allah. No such thing was written in the book of the lord. Humans had shed the tail because it was of no use, and now moved about in clothes, civilized. But the bonds had not been broken. So even though German Mian had cast off his home district of Birbhum from his life, something kept pricking him, making him ache a little. It could well be the corpse that German Mian had left behind in his village.

This part of the night was the time to read the Tahajjud namaz, which purified people's souls. It would soon be time for sehri. The intervening period between this namaz and the sehri was not very long – just like the gap between the Asr namaz of the late afternoon and the Maghrib namaz of the evening. German Mian had nothing to do now besides brooding about Pakistan. He began to muse on the seven heavens, the saat asmaan. He had come up with many an idea about this, but had never found anyone to whom he could tell them. He didn't care to write either, or else he would have written a book and given it to people to read. Conjuring up an imaginary listener sitting opposite him, German Mian began to speak about the first heaven.

'Walaqad khalaqna fawqakum sabía tara-iqa wama kunna ëani alkhalqi ghafileena...

Indeed I have created seven heavens above you, and I am not unaware of my creation.'

About to begin the story of the first one, German Mian was reminded of Miraj. Miraj was the name given to Mahanabi

Hazrat Mohammad's journey from Hatim-e-Kaabah in Mecca Sharif to Masjidul Aqsa or Baitul Mukaddas, followed by his travels through the seven heavens to reach the presence of Allahtaala. The journey from Hatim-e-Kaabah to Masjid-e-Aqsa was known as Isra, while his travels from Masjid-e-Aqsa through the seven skies to the extreme edge of the world were called Miraj. Nabiji had undertaken this journey mounted on a boraq. This vehicle moved like lightning, and was smaller than a mule but larger than a donkey. It had taken him only a few seconds to travel through the seven heavens on this fleet-footed beast. Nabiji was accompanied by two angels – Hazrat Gibrail and Hazrat Mikail.

Nabiji's voyage through the heavens was indeed a breathtaking affair. The sentries opened the door as soon as he reached the nearest heaven. Mohammad met Hazrat Adam in the first sky. There were many humans on either side of Adam. The ones on his right kept smiling, while those on his left wept continuously. Adam was observing his descendants. The people on his right had offered their faith, their Iman, before their death, but those on the left were traitors.

Not offering one's faith meant there would be no escape from tears, or was it that those who always wept had no faith to begin with, German Mian wondered. He wept too, sometimes, salty tears flowing down his cheeks. And what about the pile of skepticism he harboured within himself? Then again, he had seen many genuinely faithless traitors who always had a merry time. But all this pertained to this world they lived in.

Only after the game of life had ended would the real picture of tears and joy become evident. German Mian moved on to the tale of Nabiji's travels to the second heaven.

Here Hazrat Mohammad met Hazrat Isa and Hazrat Yahya. The Christians referred to Hazrat Isa as Jesus Christ. Isa Nabi had no father. His mother's name was Maryam, and her father's sister was Yashbi, who was much older than his mother. Yashbi became pregnant after she had passed the age for carrying a child. It was at the same time that Maryam, by Allah's powers, also became pregnant, but without being with a man. Yashbi's husband's name was Hazrat Zakaria, who was himself a prophet, and Maryam's guardian. Yashbi and Zakaria's son was Hazrat Yahya, while Maryam's son was Hazrat Isa. The two prophets who lived in the second heaven were cousins.

German Mian knew a great deal about Jesus Christ or the prophet Isa, but he had heard very little about his cousin, the prophet Yahya. A maulana had said that this prophet was extremely fond of wild honey, which could cure different kinds of illnesses. Kamrunnesa Bibi knew a lot about prophet Yahya, however. Here is what German Mian had learnt from her:

The Christians referred to this prophet as John. Prophet Yahya's mother was infertile and his father, Hazrat Zakaria, was an octogenarian. The prophet Zakaria prayed to Allah for a son at a time when both husband and wife were incapable of producing an offspring. Granting his prayer, Allah had said, 'Your son shall be named Yahya or Zakaria, a name which has never been given to anyone before.' The tomb of this prophet lay in the Ummaiya mosque in Syria.

The prophet Yahya died in most tragic circumstances. Herod Antipas, the Emperor of Rome, had an illicit relationship with his sister-in-law, his brother Herod Philip's wife, Herodias. Prophet Yahya got to know of this anti-Sharia deed. He went to the Emperor and tried to dissuade him from this sinful relationship. But the Emperor was furious with the prophet and clapped him in prison.

A few days later, Emperor Herod Antipas arranged for a feast where dancing accompanied the food and drinks offered. Herodias sent her daughter Salomé to dance at this gathering. The Emperor was delighted by the performance of his niece. Summoning Salomé, he asked, 'What do you want, my darling? I shall grant you any wish. I can even pluck the moon out of the sky for you.' Salomé asked for the head of prophet Yahya. The Emperor of Rome summoned the executioner and had the prophet beheaded so that Salomé's wish could be fulfilled.

From the second heaven Hazrat Mohammad went to the third. Here he met the most beautiful human being in the world, Hazrat Yusuf. Allahtaala had put half the beauty of the universe into creating this prophet. The prophet Yusuf welcomed Hazrat Mohammad warmly and sought blessings for him at Allah's court.

The prophet Yusuf was renowned for explaining the meaning of dreams. There would never be another like him on this earth. If such a man had been there, innumerable dreams would have been unravelled. German Mian alone had so many dreams that needed explaining! He felt overwhelmed at the mention of dreams in any discussion. This same prophet Yusuf once told his father, the prophet Yakub, 'Abbajan, in a dream I saw there were eleven planets, the sun and the moon, and all of them were showing their deference to me.' His father responded, 'Do not tell your brothers this. They will torture you. The devil is the open enemy of mankind.'

The prophet Yusuf's father also explained dreams. It was a given that by the grace of the lord his son would surpass him. The prophet's beauty caused women to fall madly in love with him. The women began to whisper that Aziz's wife Zuleikha was attracted to her young slave, that her love for him had driven her insane.

Aziz's wife invited all the women in town to a feast. Knives and forks were laid out around the plates. Everyone began to eat with their cutlery. At this time the prophet Yusuf was sent for. At the sight of him the women cut themselves with their knives. 'I swear upon the lord, he is not human,' some of them exclaimed.

But the prophet Yusuf didn't so much as glance at the women. He preferred to busy himself with his work – the tasks for which Allahtaala had sent him into the world. He freed himself from slavery by interpreting for the Emperor of Egypt a dream that he had had. Seven plump cows eating seven emaciated ones or seven green stalks standing next to seven dry ones – as he explained these dreams to the Emperor he had a premonition of bountiful harvests and famines. Prophets are visionaries who can see the future and the prophet Yusuf's explication of the Emperor's dreams had saved the entire country from the famine. Grains saved from bumper harvests ensured that people had enough to eat during the famine. Even the prophet's brothers who used to persecute him came to him asking for grains.

German Mian could not wait. He wanted to tour all seven heavens and find out about each of the prophets before it was time for the sehri. He would tell his imaginary listener the stories of the prophets in these seven heavens. So many prophets had entered the world, but not all of them had been given a special place in the seven heavens. Ascending to the fourth heaven, German Mian discovered Hazrat Mohammad meeting the prophet Idris. When the prophet was alive he would counsel people three days a week, analyzing the difference between right and wrong to guide them towards the path that led to Allah. The other four days he would devote to Ibadat Bandag for Allah. He was the first prophet to use a pen. No one knew its use before he introduced it. He would keep a close eye on the movements of the stars and planets. It was prophet Idris who began the practise of measuring and weighing things.

When prophet Idris grew very old an angel, one of his favorites, escorted him alive to paradise. Of course, the angel did this on Allah's instructions, for angels had no free will. It astonished the angel of death to see the prophet Idris in paradise. How could he be here when he hadn't died? But once the prophet entered paradise, however, he did have to give his life to the malak-ul-maut, the angel of death.

Now German Mian recounted the story of Hazrat Mohammad's visit to the fifth heaven. Allah's most trustworthy servant Hazrat Haroun was to be found here. He was Hazrat Musa's brother. Allah had always declared him the victor. Prophet Haroun had joined his brother Musa in his holy war. He was an extraordinary orator. People would stop in their tracks when they heard him speak, wonder writ large on their faces. When the country was being terrorized by Firawn, Pharaoh Rameses II, it was the prophet Musa who put an end to the tyranny, with the prophet Haroun as his companion. However, it would be wrong to imagine that he did nothing but accompany the prophet Musa. He had been granted a place in the fifth heaven because of his magnificent achievements. During the night of his Miraj, Hazrat Mohammad was captivated by the prophet Haroun's beauty. Hazrat Mohammad had compared Ali to the prophet Haroun, although Hazrat Ali was not a prophet. Hazrat Mohammad's relationship with Hazrat Ali was similar to Musa's with Haroun. There was a shrine to prophet Haroun in Jabal Haroun in Egypt.

There were two heavens to go. German Mian's thoughts shifted to the story of Hazrat Mohammad's journey to the sixth heaven. Prophet Musa, the prophet Haroun's brother, was here – a prophet to everyone, Jews, Christians and Muslims. German Mian sensed many similarities between Hazrat Mohammad and the prophet Musa. Both of them were simultaneously prophet and messenger, as were Hazrat Isa and the prophet Daud. They were not only Allah's messengers but also the ones to whom the divine book was revealed. Hazrat Mohammad's meeting with the prophet Musa was an important event in his life. Had this meeting not taken place, no one would have come to know about the five namazes. Because Allahtaala was compassionate, he informed Hazrat Mohammad about the five namazes through this encounter and that was how everyone in the world came to know about it. The Quran Sharif contains more than five hundred references to the prophet Musa. There was another prophet who was his contemporary, his name was Hazrat Khizir. Not only did prophet Musa meet him, but they also held many secret conclaves. German Mian did not want to bring up their conversations, for that would take up the rest of the night. He had just one more thing to say before leaving the sixth heaven. As evidence of his prophethood, Hazrat Musa had demonstrated two miracles or mojza, one of which was a favourite of German Mian's.

The Emperor of Egypt had declared, 'O Musa! If you have a miracle to perform, show us. That is, if you are indeed a truthful man.'

Whereupon Musa released his stick and it turned into a serpent.

In the seventh heaven Hazrat Mohammad met Hazrat Ibrahim. German Mian had read about Hazrat Ibrahim in different places in the Quran Sharif. When reading the namaz, the Durood Sharif had to be read in honour of this prophet. Reading the Durood-e-Ibrahim boosted one's balance of good deeds. In this Durood of the namaz, Ibrahim was the only person who was spoken of other than Hazrat Mohammad. The prophet Ibrahim had repaired Allah's chamber at Kaa'ba. He was vehemently opposed to idol worship. One day, Hazrat Ibrahim visited his father Azar, a staunch idol-worshipper. The prophet asked his father without hesitation, 'How can you pray to those stones, Abbajaan?' A furious Azar told the prophet Ibrahim to control himself.

On another occasion Ibrahim entered a temple and discovered several idols in it. He proceeded to break them one by one. Before leaving, he embedded his axe – which he had used to demolish the idols – in the shoulder of one of the largest idols. It did not take long for the priests to come to know about what he had done. Prophet Ibrahim tried to explain to them that idols that could not even save themselves could not possibly be expected to save others. The idol-worshippers were so incensed that they made a fire-pit and cast Ibrahim into it. Hazrat Ibrahim spent forty days in those flames. For Ibrahim's sake Allahtaala had made the fire as pleasing as flowers.

German Mian knew that Ibrahim lived in the highest of the heavens. Allah had given him this honour. On the instruction of Allah this prophet had been ready to sacrifice his favourite son Ismail. Then Allahtaala sent a ram instead of Ibrahim's son to the altar, and eventually the beast was sacrificed. This was how Allahtaala banished the execrable tradition of human sacrifice prevalent in Arab countries, substituting it with the sacrifice of rams. The thought of human sacrifice terrified German Mian. A Dutch artist Rembrandt had painted the scene of Ibrahim sacrificing his son. German Mian had frozen at the sight of a photograph of the painting. The thought of it still sent shivers down his spine.

Allah's throne was situated above the seven heavens. Next to him was seated Allahtaala's habib, his beloved, Hazrat Mohammad. German Mian knew that no other human being could reach this place; no one had even mastered the language capable of describing it. A miraculous tree existed above the seven heavens. Its name was Sidrat al-Muntaha, the Lote Tree. Humans knew little about this tree, located at the extreme edge of the physical world. There could have been a divine oracle, of course – but that was a different matter.

There wasn't much time left for the sehri. German Mian decided to go to the dining room even as he tried to recollect how sweet the ambrosial fruit of the Sidrat al-Muntaha was to taste.

~ *Jannat-ul-Khulad* ~

THE ETERNAL GARDEN

On the fourteenth of August 1947 the country became independent. The districts of Murshidabad and Malda had indeed been allotted to Pakistan. German Mian's dream-sickness was not bothering him much. Nor was there any sign of his dreams on his face. German Mian continued to feel as though a dervish – neither man nor woman (at least it was impossible to tell from the voice) – this person in a strange attire, was telling him in a voice that did not betray its gender, 'It's a day of celebration for you. The flag of Pakistan will fly atop your house, a green flag, with the moon and stars.'

German Mian retrieved one of the dreams he had stored away. It was the time of the birth of Kamrunnesa's first child. When his wife's labour pain was peaking, German Mian felt a violent tug in his bowels. The men's toilet was a long distance from the house. As he was on his way there with a mug, he saw a young man standing on the bank of the pond by the toilet. At first German Mian mistook him for one of the local youths. But in the half-light of dawn he clearly saw that the man's elbows, knees and ankles were all turned inwards. Or, it would be more appropriate to say that his face seemed to be pointing backwards. When German Mian called out to the man he began to walk, his face towards German Mian. But the distance between German Mian and the man with the knees and ankles turned inwards kept increasing. German Mian was brought home unconscious. When he recovered he was given the news of the birth of his first child. Then the doctor arrived, and he was given medicine and food. But the dream refused to leave him. German Mian did not know whether to call it a dream or something else that occurred in an intermediate state between a dream and wakefulness. But he realized clearly that the man whose elbows and knees and ankles faced backwards actually wanted to come up to him. The closer he tried to get to German Mian, the more the distance between them seemed to increase.

These thoughts ran through his head while German Mian watched the neighbourhood boys flying their pigeons.

Was it even possible to keep track of the different varieties of pigeons in the world? Among the pigeons that were airborne or pecking at grains inside their pens were breeds like the Sheth, Dhali, Jag, Lili, Piling, Chhatia, Gola, Laksha, Shirazi, Kagazi, Notonand Giribaz. So many different names, and each with a specific meaning. Bowler Sahib of Behrampore was very fond of pigeons. German Mian had seen other varieties in Behrampore, most of them foreign. There was a breed with curled wings named Frillback. The Jacobins had masses of feathers on their heads. Strassers resembled doves. The Fantails indeed had tails like fans.

Among the pigeons in the sky now was a breed called Homer. These pigeons participated in competitions, for they could fly swiftly. The local breed, Gola, was quick too but could not fly for very long. The Lakhshas and the Shirazs were fragile – they died unless they were meticulously cared for. The Kagazis sent a shiver down the spine with their appearance – white all over but ink-black around the eyes. It was impossible to list all the varieties – Ekbaz, Dobaz, Balparda, Jagbablu, Nagot, King, Prince, Potter, Chila, Masakali. German Mian had once wanted to own pigeons. His elder brother had said that it was not an auspicious whim for it adversely affected a family's fortunes. German Mian had heard that the pigeons of Medina that were at death's doorstep somehow flew to Mecca and circled the Kaa'ba before falling into the arms of death. They might be pigeons, but even they knew the necessity of circling the Kaa'ba before they died. And yet rich people did not go on the Haj. Why couldn't they do what even the pigeons of Medina could? May Allah Tabaraktaala grant everyone the ability to go on the Haj. He had heard this story about the pigeons of Medina from Badreddoza, not that either German Mian or Badreddoza knew whether the story was true. But he simply could not understand why pigeons were being made to fly on the day of independence. Did the pigeons know that they too were now inhabitants of Pakistan? Pet pigeons were usually let loose to fly in the late afternoon, so there must be some objective behind their being made to fly so early in the morning. What if they flew westward now? They would reach Agardanga in Burdwan; Burdwan was not free yet. The Giribaj pigeons were turning somersaults in the sky. It was a wonderful sight. The Notons couldn't do that, they only turned somersaults on the ground.

Watching the flight paths of the pigeons, German Mian was reminded of a dream. In the middle of a terrifying dream he could not find water although he was very thirsty. He needed to perform wuzu. Discovering a mound of earth behind a mosque he had tried to run his hand over it in an attempt at dry ablutions. This was the rule when water was not available – it was as good as performing wuzu. But as soon as he touched it, three birds emerged. Were they Ababil birds or pigeons? They might be Hoopoes too. Were they Suleiman Nabi's pet birds, with whom he was known to talk? The three birds that had come out of the mound began to converse amongst themselves. German Mian realized that these birds resembling pigeons were not from this world. They gradually took the form of distorted maps. Taking their clothes off they began to bathe in blood, after which they were transformed into humans. All these different breeds of pigeons were flying around today – were they also from another world, another land? Till yesterday they had belonged to another country. Even now they could reach this other country after just a few minutes of flight. And they needn't return to Pakistan if they didn't want to. Yes, Pakistan. German Mian could not say it enough; the district of Murshidabad now belonged to Pakistan. Millions of people like him had been waiting for this day and finally it had dawned.

Presently German Mian spotted Majid Khondkar, Hafiz Molla, Badreddoza and others near the pigeon pen. All of them were here to see the pigeons. It couldn't be said with certainty that Majid Khondkar was delighted by the formation of Pakistan. Hafiz Molla's expression suggested he had got all the property owned by the Hindus in Harinya dirt cheap. 'What do you make of all this, Mian?' German Mian asked Badreddoza, who looked grim. 'What can I make of it? I'm thinking of horses. Of calculating the number of horses.'

German Mian could surmise what Badreddoza's conundrum would be. Badreddoza continued without a pause, 'A boy named Farid was told by his father as he was about to die. Farid here are my seventeen horses, and there are three of you brothers. You will take half the horses, give two-thirds of the remaining ones to your elder brother, and one-third of the rest to your little brother. Farid knew arithmetic. He could add a horse to the seventeen to fulfill his father's mathematical wishes, but can our Congress and Muslim League people do that? How could Murshidabad and Malda go to Pakistan? I'm told Pakistan's flag is flying over the Hazarduari. After fighting for the Congress and Hindustan all his life Nawab Wasef Ali Mirza had to finally unfurl the flag of Pakistan! The calculations don't add up, Mian.'

Hafiz Molla could contain himself no longer. Loudly, he said 'They are the descendants of Mir Zafar. Do you remember him? The traitor on whose instructions the Nawab of Bengal, Bihar and Orissa was murdered. Wasef Ali Mirza is from that family, and he made his son Kasem Ali Mirza join the Muslim League while he stayed with the Congress, pretending to be a friend of the Hindus. Another descendant of that family, Iskandar Mirza, is also moving to Pakistan to be a nawab there. What they want is power – it does not matter to them whether it is in Pakistan or Hindustan.'

German Mian didn't care for such conversation. He could not tolerate anybody who slandered others. Besides, he respected Kasem Ali Mirza greatly. He needed to find out what the Hindus of this area were thinking. He would have to go to Zulfikar Mian to find out the truth. Then he would take him along to Harinya to see the amusing plight of the Hindus with his own eyes.

After Iftar that evening, he went to Zulfikar Mian's house. He ran into Mian outside the front room. As on the first day they had met, Zulfiqar Ali asked German Husain, 'Do you know the name of the star you see there in the Qibla sky that points towards Mecca?'

Looking at the star in the western sky, German Mian replied, 'Yes, that's Al-Zohra.'

'That's not the point. I know its name is Al-Zohra. How did that star appear on the flag of Pakistan?'

'I have no idea.'

'The five-pointed star is the symbol of the five pillars of Islam. Kalema, namaz, Roja, Jakat, Haj.'

'Then what will the Hindus do? Or is there no room for Hindus in Pakistan? Muslims will live in Hindustan too.'

'Don't panic, Mianbhai. Look at the flag closely. The dark green section of the flag on the far side of the pole symbolizes Islam. The white near the pole stands for the minority non-Muslims in Pakistan. Hindus are non-Muslims, aren't they? Or do you have objections about that too?'

'No, I have no objections, but will the Hindus here accept Pakistan? Has anyone talked it over with them?'

'There's no use, Mian. Not everything can be done taking the best interests of people into account. Tell me...Your brother is in Birbhum, isn't he? If he can accept Hindustan, why shouldn't the Hindus here accept Pakistan?'

German Mian didn't understand clearly what Zulfiqar Ali was saying. He sensed, however, that the Hindus here were not happy. All of them were considering abandoning their homes in Murshidabad. Why should that be the case? Why should people have to leave their homes, their land? They were humans too. It was different if they were going by choice. At one point they had thought Murshidabad would not be part of Pakistan, that it would remain in Hindustan. Now Pakistan would be ruled by the Muslim League. Whom could they trust if they stayed on here? How many Muslims would be willing to live in India if it were to be run by the Hindu Mahasabha? German Mian had himself been a Congress supporter once.

But he too had shouted himself hoarse for the formation of Pakistan as demanded by the League. Yet he could not accept that Hindus should leave.

German Mian felt despondent when he left Zulfiqar Mian's house. On the road he wondered whether he should meet the Hindus around here on his own and talk to them; but they would be suspicious of him. You settled down here in Murshidabad in the hope of living in Pakistan, and now you're here to mock us Hindus for being forced to abandon our homes. No, he'd better not go. German Mian had no wish to be cursed by the people. He should get back home before it got late, or else he would have to stomach his wife's invectives. Apparently it wasn't safe. The new government existed only on paper. No police force had been created. The country was technically independent, but actually it was still under British rule.

The subject came up after dinner. When Kamrunnesa's nephew said, as he always did, 'Riots are inevitable, no one can stop them,' German Mian asked his wife, 'How are things? Murshidabad is part of Pakistan now.'

Kamrunnesa smiled. 'Wait for a day or two, Mian sahib. Then you'll know which areas are going to Pakistan and which to India.'

'What do you mean?'

'If all Muslim-majority areas go to Pakistan and Hindu-majority areas to India, how can Chittagong be a part of Pakistan? It's neither Muslim-majority nor Hindu-majority. Sir

Cyril Radcliffe is still drawing up the rules for the allotment. Wait for a day or two, Mian.'

'You mean the country will be repartitioned? We're flying the flag of Pakistan here, but will Murshidabad not remain part of Pakistan then?'

'I don't know. I've heard Pakistan wants the Hindu-majority district of Khulna and India doesn't want to let go of Murshidabad. If they agree what can you and I do? Sir Cyril is very thick with Mountbatten and the Congress has Mountbatten under its thumb. If the Congress wants to keep Malda and Murshidabad in India, who can stop them?'

German Mian was enraged. 'How will it harm the Congress to have Murshidabad in Pakistan?'

Like a seasoned political expert Kamrunnesa said, 'I hear India needs Malda so that Darjeeling and Jalpaiguri are not cut off. And Murshidabad and Nadia are needed to protect the Hooghly river. Atul Gupta of Tangail is battling over this. My friend was here a few days ago – she told me all this. This partition is the agony of hell, Mian Sahib. The number of people who will cross over, who will lose their homes, is beyond count. You mustn't lose your head over this. Whatever Allahtaala thinks best will happen. Now go to bed quickly or else you won't be up in time for sehri.'

German Mian went to bed. He didn't expect to get much sleep. He would pass the night in a haze.

In the state between sleep and wakefulness, German Mian was no longer a human – he turned into a slow-paced snail.

His soft body, protected by a shell, inched across land and water. And with this body he sensed the presence of a corpse which he had left behind in his village. In his dream the body of the dead woman lengthened, and German Mian in the form of a snail looked for a wound on it. The throat would have turned blue had she been throttled to death, while a battered corpse would have had a reddish hue. But since colours cannot be discerned in dreams and the snail has no more than two senses, it could not experience anything but the touch of the corpse and the indescribable taste of death. German Mian felt the lack of the remaining senses in his dream. Had he been a bee he would have been able to see the disfigured face of the dead woman, which had rotted by now. He climbed the dead body in the form of a snail, realizing that this corpse was in fact the entire world, which a snail could not hope to traverse in its entirety. And yet it was this impossible task on which he had been forced to embark. Just like sleep, dreams too have several levels. Moving up and down between these stages and levels, German Mian became thirsty. About to pick up the glass of water near his head, he discovered it was soft, warm and fluffy. It could even be a furry creature. It said 'meow' as soon as he touched it, and retreated to a distance. At once a blue glow played over the room. German Mian was flabbergasted. His astonishment peaked when the cat asked in a human voice, 'Don't you want to have your sehri, Mianbhai?'

German Mian recognized the voice. It belonged to the badshah of jinns, Jul Jenahen. It wasn't clear why he was back.

German Mian was not afraid of him anymore. The badshah of jinns had been hovering nearby for some time now.

'I am Jul. The badshah of jinns. I have a request for you, my lord.'

'A request?'

'I'll tell you later. But listen to me first. My name is Jul Jenahen. Sulaiman Nabi's father King Daud killed my brother Amrud. He was a loveable but naughty child. He has a son named Fasif. A beautiful boy whose father is dead. It is my dream that you make him your servant. I'm going now. I'll be back. Think it over.'

German Mian knew that if a jinn were to become a man's slave, he could achieve the impossible; there was nothing that an enslaved jinn could not do. If German Mian were to make Fasif his slave would he be able to keep Murshidabad in Pakistan? The jinn could tear up all of Radcliffe's papers. Was it possible? Waking up for his sehri, German Mian realized he couldn't afford to sleep anymore. It was the day of India's independence. A little study, a little perusal of the Quran and Haadith was better than sleeping on such a day.

After sehri, he opened the book to find out how to meet his objectives in this life and the next:

Honest Muslims should not have the purpose of fulfilling earthly desires, hankering for the luxuries of the world and unnecessary wealth that makes one forget one's Akhirat, one's afterlife. It is not inappropriate to harbour desires that are linked to the afterlife. So every Muslim who follows the true path can wish for improvement in the world of righteousness. The kalemas below are particularly effective for this. Uttering these respectfully after the Farz namaz every day would be excellent.

First, read one hundred times: La Ilaha Illallah al-Malikul Haqqul Mubin. There is no power except Allah, the King, the Right, the Manifest.

To make a jinn or spirit appear, to treat illnesses and to keep a jinn under one's control or to force obedience on him requires extreme courage and patience. Losing heart when attempting to achieve these is fraught with comparable or a higher degree of danger. It may even lead to death. Therefore, one must mould oneself with arduous devotion and unrelenting hard work, all the while remaining conscious of every aspect of preparation.

Next, German Mian proceeded to read. 'How to counteract the advent and infestation of jinns at home.' He felt fearful about reading the chapter on 'Making jinns and spirits appear through forty days of retreating into isolation and bringing them under one's control'. When he finished reading, it was time for the azaan of Fazr. Finishing his namaz he went to bed.

German Mian was awakened by Badreddoza, who brought news of the dire crisis that Aman Mian from Agardanga in Burdwan district found himself in. The formation of Pakistan had been formalized a day earlier; the formation of India, today. The men's toilet outside Aman Mian's house was on the border of Murshidabad and Burdwan. People said that using the toilet meant setting one foot in Murshidabad and one in Burdwan. With the two districts now in two separate countries, Aman Mian was in deep trouble. How was he to clear his bowels in the morning straddling two countries? The border security forces would demolish his cherished toilet in a few days. Much of his land also fell across the border between the two districts. Half of one of his lakes was in Burdwan and the other half in Murshidabad. No one knew what the fate of all this property was to be. He could not find anyone to whom he could transfer the portions in Murshidabad. All eyes were on his latrine.

German Mian did not know whether to laugh or cry. Everyone knew that the partition had forced many people to forsake their homes but the kind of crisis that Aman Mian was in, having to straddle two countries every morning when he went for a shit, was unprecedented. If the Radcliffe Mission were to change its ruling Aman Mian's strange crisis could be dispelled.

German Mian could sense how the people of Murshidabad were changing. Originally there were many people on Wasef Ali Mirza's side, not in favour of the creation of Pakistan. No sooner had the flag of Pakistan been hoisted than the Muslims of Murshidabad started raising slogans in support of Pakistan. If so many people were voicing their demand no power could keep this district out of Pakistan. Muslim League leaders like Abul Hashem were still conducting meetings and processions at different places in support of Pakistan. They were doing their best to secure the support of the people so that their demand for Pakistan's share was not ignored, but Suhrawardy was still silent. He had once declared that if Pakistan were created he would have one foot in India and one in Pakistan. If that was the truth he should be found in Aman Mian's toilet right now.

The day passed in this manner. The real news began to flow in the next day, Saturday. No one had shopped for Eid this time. Neither had German Mian. People were wondering which country they would be living in – and whether they would have to move from one country to another. No one was bothered about Eid. They were all worried about what the Radcliffe Mission would announce. Eid was a day or two away. Arrangements for viewing the moon would start in the evening. Once the moon was spotted, the next day would be declared Eid.

They had heard that it wasn't just east and west Bengal; the same problem had cropped up in some areas of Punjab as well. Sir Cyril had accepted the Congress's arguments and acknowledging the importance of the districts of Nadia and Murshidabad he had allotted both to India. Or else ships would not be able to enter the Calcutta port. India would build a dam in Murshidabad to keep the Calcutta port alive. What Kamrunnesa Bibi had said about Malda district had also proved a hundred per cent correct. India needed Malda to ensure a passage to and from Jalpaiguri and Darjeeling. They had got the district. Meanwhile, thousands of people had become incensed with the news of Murshidabad being restored to India. Many of the inhabitants of Nadia were also in favour of Pakistan, they had taken out processions on the streets. From tomorrow, the seventeenth of August, Sunday, the flag of India would start flying in all these places. The Hindus had begun their victory processions in several parts of the district. Riots could erupt again. No one knew whether Wasef Ali Mirza was pleased or not, but he would have to take Pakistan's moon-and-stars flag down from the spire of Hazarduari and unfurl India's tricolor in its place. Apparently he had already placed orders for the Indian flag. Wasef Mirza's son Kasem Ali was downcast. Iskandar Mirza had already moved from Murshidabad to Karachi.

On Sunday, the seventeenth of August, Murshidabad returned to India. A delighted Majid Khondkar said, 'The boy is back home where he belongs.' People observed with great surprise that Badreddoza looked extremely dejected. Hafiz Molla had stopped eating. Zulfikar Mian was holed up at home. German Mian found himself back in the grip of evil dreams. Would he have to wind up here and go back to his old village? He had moved to Murshidabad because it was to become a part of Pakistan. If he had no choice but to live in India, why should he stay here? He might as well go back to his own home. It was best to return to one's roots.

On the evening of seventeenth August, the Eid moon became visible. Jinnah Sahib addressed the nation:

'This is our first Eid immediately following in the heralding of free independent sovereign Pakistan having been established. This day of rejoicing throughout the Muslim world so aptly comes immediately in the wake of our national state being established, and therefore, it is a matter of special significance and happiness to us all. I wish on this auspicious day a very happy Eid to all Muslims wherever they may be throughout the world – an Eid that will usher in, I hope, a new era of prosperity and will mark the onward march of renaissance of Islamic culture and ideals. I fervently pray that God Almighty make us all worthy of our past and hoary history and give us strength to make Pakistan truly a great nation amongst all the nations of the world. No doubt we have achieved Pakistan, but that is only yet the beginning of an end. Great responsibilities have come to us, and equally great should be our determination and endeavor to discharge them, and the fulfillment thereof will demand of us efforts and sacrifices in the cause, no less for construction and building of our nation than what was required for the achievement of the cherished goal of Pakistan. The time for real solid work has now arrived, and I have no doubt in my mind that the Muslim genius will put its shoulder to the wheel and conquer all obstacles in our way on the road, which may appear uphill.

Let us not, on this occasion, forget those of our brethren and sisters who have sacrificed their all, so that Pakistan may be established and we may live. We fervently pray that their souls may rest in peace and we shall never forget the memory of those who are no more and those who have suffered.

For many, Eid will be not an occasion of such great joy and rejoicing as in Pakistan. Those of our brethren who are minorities in Hindustan may rest assured that we shall never neglect or forget them. Our hearts go out to them, and we shall consider no effort too great to help them and secure their well-being, for I recognize that it is the Muslim minority provinces in this sub-continent who were the pioneers and carried the banner aloft for the achievement of our cherished goal of Pakistan. I shall never forget their support, nor I hope the majority provinces in Pakistan will fail to appreciate that they were the pioneers in the vanguard of our historic and heroic struggle for the achievement of Pakistan, which today is an accomplished fact.'

~ Jannat-ul-Firdaus ~

THE HIGHEST SPOT

After considering the matter calmly, Runa's Nana German Mian decided to leave Murshidabad. The people would go first, followed by their belongings. Mulla Badreddoza was given the responsibility for taking care of his house after his departure. An awning was set up on the ox-cart. A thick bedding was laid out. Since German Mian was a man who liked his luxuries, it was decided that he would take a radio along and listen to music on the way, but his radio had stopped working a few days ago and hadn't been repaired. If they left the area at midnight, they would be at their village in about four hours. To dispel the darkness of the night, a lantern was hung beneath the cart. The cart had a new driver, German Mian's coachman Tentuli having died suddenly a few days ago.

This new man was strangely dressed. He constantly spouted stories. He looked like a fakir or a pir, but his face was not distinct. It was covered, along with his head, by the sort of shawl which those who had been to Mecca wrapped around their heads. Only his eyes were visible – such enchanting eyes. German Mian did not know where his brother had found this coachman.

The man spoke of a berry tree as he drove. Its fruit was sweeter than the fruits of paradise. It was called 'sidra' in Arabic. When this coachman didn't even know Bangla well enough, how could he know Arabic? German Mian had heard that long devotion to Allah and his messenger gave one mastery over certain aspects of secret knowledge. When he saw and heard this coachman, he felt that he was privy to some such secret ontology. Which was why he could say knowledgeably about the tree named Sidrat al-Muntaha, 'It is difficult for humans to know what the berry tree, which is to be found beyond the seventh sky at the extreme edge of the material world, is like and what its real nature and characteristics are.'

Sumai the coachman also held forth on the ambrosial fruit of the Lote tree. It took a hundred and fifty human years to go from the roots of these trees to their highest branches. Mankind had not yet succeeded in constructing transportation to travel from the first heaven to the second. And yet Nabiji, the finest among men, went there riding a buraq, a fleet-footed animal smaller than a mule but larger than a donkey. Mounted on this beast which moved like lightning Nabiji ascended to every successive level of the seven heavens and even higher in an instant on the night of the Miraj. Studded with gems, these steps were not like those of this world. Atop the seventh heaven Nabiji had seen a miraculous tree – the Sidrat al-Muntaha. Only fourteen specific people were allowed to step into its shade – Hazrat Mohammad, his daughter Fatima Zohra, and the twelve Imams from Imam Ali to Imam Mehdi. For everyone else in the world there was the shade of the banyan tree. Those to whom even this was denied died trying to shield the rice from the sun.

German Mian had never heard the story of these fourteen people being allowed into the shade of the tree. Was it divinely ordained that he must hear everything? It was now. Sumai the coachman began to reel off page after page of ontology about the leaves and fruits of this tree. And the cart lurched on at a violent speed.

The faster the vehicle moved, the more shadowy Sumai seemed to become. Among the things he had begun to recount were many events from German Mian's own life. How had he come to know of these secrets? German Mian encouraged him to talk. Driving the cart with extraordinary skill, he said that Jul Jenahen was the badshah of the jinns. He was in deep trouble over a granddaughter and a nephew of his. Despite being the children of jinns, they were clamoring to live in human houses. Jul had approached various people, only to be disappointed. No one was willing to accommodate his granddaughter and nephew. Sumai the coachman also mentioned the woman behind the purdah whom German Mian had seen through the south-facing window in the house in Murshidabad, working or pretending to work on the opposite bank of the pond. The only thing Sumai had not mentioned yet was the corpse whom German Mian had left behind in his own village on the day he had moved to Murshidabad.

Sumai the coachman wished to say many things about jinns.

They had lived on earth well before human beings arrived here. Devout Muslims had no choice but to acknowledge jinns because the Quran mentioned them. If someone were to deny the existence of jinns they were actually denying the Quran. Even if humans could not see jinns the jinns, could see humans. A jinn became an adult only at the age of three hundred. Once, a meteor shower was used to prevent them from getting any news from the sky. The jinns grew very worried about this. They sent their representatives to the east and west, to every nook and cranny on earth. Their question: what was the matter, why couldn't they hear the news anymore? When the representatives dispatched to Heja reached a place named Nakhal, Hazrat Mohammad was reading the Fazr namaz along with his companions. When they heard the Quran being read during the namaz they swore, 'This kalaam is the obstacle that is preventing us from gathering news from the skies.' Returning, they disclosed everything to their people and said, 'We have hearkened the most singular Quran. Allahtaala has apprised his messenger of all these incidents through his Ayat.'

This was the first time that Runa's Nana German Mian had set eyes on Sumai the coachman. He had been told that Sumai lived in the next village. When Tentuli suddenly died, Mejo Mian was at first unable to find a trustworthy replacement. You had to trust your coachman. This man had apparently appeared from nowhere, provided considerable evidence of his trustworthiness, and started work. German Mian had no idea how a man who resembled a pir or fakir could also be a coachman. Sumai the coachman was reluctant to stop talking. He also proved zealous about offering details of not just jinns, but also of the origin of the universe, of the seven heavens and the level above them. German Mian asked him about corpses. He replied:

'There are many strange and secret things,
Fiery and irresistible, hidden in a murder
Listen to my core advice, my little man
The world is colourful and you are a child.'

This was the exhortation that German Mian had heard at the shrine of Makhdum Sahib. But where had Sumai the coachman come across such sophisticated ideas? He could not be an ordinary man. His powers were undoubtedly potent. German Mian's astonishment deepened. He also began to feel fearful, and started reading the Ayatul Kursi. If you read this particular part of the chapter and drew a circle around yourself, no evil jinn or nymph could come near you. But Sumai the coachman was human. Why then was German Mian afraid of him? Reading the Ayatul Kursi repeatedly, he tried to reconstruct the face of the corpse. There were nine creatures in or near the cart now. German Mian, Kamrunnesa Bibi, Sumai the coachman, German Mian's two daughters, Kamrunnesa's nephew, and the two black oxen. Everyone besides the oxen, German Mian and Sumai the coachman were asleep. Not that the wakefulness of the oxen was clearly discernible in the darkness. Sumai the coachman talked to them too. Was that the sound of a tenth creature breathing that German Mian could hear? The sound seemed to remind him even more strongly of the dead woman. Somebody or some people had killed her and left her in front of the school. Or was it a natural death? Then how would the corpse have made it to the school? German Mian did not know where, or if at all, she had been buried.

The tenth creature, whose presence Runa's Nana German Mian couldn't quite ascertain, seemed to be cutting through the darkness to accompany their cart like a guard. It whirled about, alternately settling above the awning and circling the lantern. This was the young angel to whom hidden powers had assigned the task of looking after German Mian. German Mian watched Sumai the coachman drive the cart. The oxen were galloping at a furious pace. At this rate they would be home before daybreak.

The village to which German Mian was going was his own village. He recalled many different things as he approached it. Shortly before the famine, a sudden increase in the price of coarse rice from two annas per kilogram to four had forced poor people to starve themselves as well as their children. Three of Tentuli's five children died of malnutrition. The poor fellow had died too. News of deaths reached him frequently after he moved to Murshidabad. Someone or the other was starving to death every day and in the midst of these series of deaths came independence. People all over were without food. Meanwhile, rows of flags were fluttering. There was an exodus from India to Pakistan, many people were coming across from the other side too. This migration was the outcome of independence.

German Mian did not know what resulted in the starvation all around him. Hundreds of famished people descended on the fields to collect slugs that were left behind after the taro roots had been collected. German Mian had seen this for himself. He couldn't bear to witness the suffering of poor people over the lack of food. It wasn't clear what independence meant to these people. If freedom had meant that they would have enough to eat, that would have been meaningful, no matter which country they lived in – Pakistan or Hindustan. Could a governor or a group of people possibly ensure that they got food? And yet one class of people had immense wealth at their disposal. The production of rice was falling and imports had been stopped. People across the world had spent billions to buy arms for a World War. As though they were performing the last rites of their father, neglecting which would mean being ostracized by other villagers and burning in the fires of hell. Even now carts were piled high with rice in the dead of the night and dispatched to the city. But those who grew rice starved. Growing rice was no easy matter. From sowing and weeding to harvesting, a hundred and eight different kind of hard labour were involved. But inevitably it was those who grew the rice who died of starvation. The British government had not bothered about this all this time, could the government of the independent country prevent this? German Mian saw no ray of hope.

Whether on Sumai's orders or not, the oxen were racing at breakneck speed now. German Mian was rattled to the bones but there was a unique pleasure in travelling at this speed. At this rate it would take another half an hour to get home. German Mian could see many graves on either side of the road in the half-light. This was not a new sight, but it seemed to him that most of the graves were fresh. The famine had long passed; nor had people from this area died in the World War. Then where had all these graves sprung from? Was this Khudataala's wonder? German Mian asked Sumai the coachman.

Sumai offered an explanation. Those who had succumbed to the famine had obviously died, but those who had survived had just about survived without actually dying. They were in worse shape than corpses. Malnutrition and disease did not allow them to fight for very long. In any case, famines and plagues were permanent fixtures in the homes of the poor. All these people had dreamt of was about getting two square meals a day once the country was independent. But they had died before their dreams could either come true or be proved false. These graves belonged to them.

Now Runa's Nana, German Mian, was close to his village. There – the school was in sight! The village would begin after they passed the school, and German Mian's house was a little further down the road. He moved ahead, leaving behind his family graveyard on the left. Muttering, 'Assalamo alaikum ahalul kabar – peace be upon you, my family in your graves,' he noticed that there were fresh graves here as well. Responding to German Mian's questioning look, Sumai said that the poor people's graveyards were full, which was why they had been forced to take shelter in the cemeteries of rich people like German Mian. Sumai the coachman suddenly leapt off the cart, surprising German Mian. The cart lurched to a halt. Pointing to the cemetery in the half-light, he began, 'There's Harun Sheikh, there's Rahim Zola, next to him Same Ali, and then...' The names would not stop rolling off Sumai the coachman's tongue. They were innumerable. The last name that he pronounced terrified German Mian. At any other time he would have fainted. But his wife and children were on the cart. Who would take them home? Having pointed out his own grave Sumai disappeared somewhere. Picking up the coachman's stick, German Mian proceeded to drive the cart himself. He would somehow have to cover the remaining distance home. German Mian, coachman now, goaded the oxen onward. Yet Kamrunnesa, behind her purdah, remained unaware of all of this.